CROSSING'S REDEMPTION

CARRIE DAWS

IMMEASURABLE
WORKS

CROSSING'S REDEMPTION

© 2014 by Carrie Daws

All rights reserved

Printed in the United States of America

ISBN: 978-0-9981678-7-9

eISBN: 978-0-998678-6-2

Cover design by Matthew Mulder

Page Layout by Carrie Daws

IMMEASURABLE WORKS

104 Harvest Ln.

Raeford, NC 28376, USA

Heal me, Lord, and I will be healed;
save me and I will be saved,
for you are the one I praise.

Jeremiah 17:14

CHAPTER 1

*A*MBER YAGER PULLED HER 2010 black Jeep Liberty off Highway 26 at Crossing, Oregon. Running her hand through her dark hair, she rested her slender arm on the console between the front seats. "We're almost home, baby boy."

She looked in the rearview mirror to see the reflection of six-month old Daniel in the mirror fastened above his rear-facing car seat. He had fallen asleep shortly after leaving the doctor's office in Portland an hour ago, and his chubby cheeks and closed eyes weren't showing any signs of waking now. The May sun coming through her window warmed her enough that she didn't have to worry too much about constantly adjusting the heat in the Jeep. She liked it warm, but the child did not like being too hot.

She turned right onto Hood Street and thought about stopping in the town square to see her parents who helped run the local hardware store. "Not sure I'm ready for all of Dad's questions about the appointment today, God." His journalistic mind frequently took over in conversations, and today she feared he'd seek answers she wasn't sure she had. She drove by the two-story building, vowing to call her mom soon.

Just as Amber approached the turn-off that would take her a short distance out of town to the home she shared with her husband, Peter, she noticed Patricia Guire sitting on her front porch steps. Amber raised her hand in greeting, but the sixty-six-year-old woman barely acknowledged her.

That's odd, thought Amber. *She's usually friendly to me.*

She braked in front of Patricia's home and rolled down her window. "Hi, Mrs. Guire," she called out. "How are you?"

Patricia barely lifted her hand in response.

Amber tried again. "Are you okay, Mrs. Guire?" She barely heard the response.

"Fine."

Amber watched for a moment, trying to decide what to do. Patricia's short, gray hair blew slightly with the breeze, but the rest of her was uncommonly still. *Something's not right, Lord.*

Go help, came a gentle response.

Amber pulled into the driveway and put the Jeep into park. Leaving it running and hoping Daniel would sleep for a while still, Amber grabbed her phone and got out of the vehicle. Patricia didn't look her way.

Amber crouched one step below Patricia and looked up into her face. Thankfully, most of the porch was in the afternoon shade. "What's wrong, Mrs. Guire?"

"I...just need...a moment," she said breathlessly. "I'll be... fine...in a minute."

Amber unlocked her phone and went to her contacts list. She clicked on her brother's work number. "I'm calling Ryan."

Her brother being a licensed EMT had come in handy several times over the last few years, but she was now just as thankful that Mrs. Guire lived only a few blocks from the town clinic where he was working to become a physician's assistant.

The receptionist answered on the second ring. "Crossing Clinic."

"Hey, Becka. It's Amber. Sorry to be short but I have a problem. Is Ryan there?"

"Yeah. He's just finishing up with a patient. Do you want to hold?"

"No," said Amber. "Please have him meet me at Mrs. Guire's house. Tell him I need him now."

Amber ended the call and picked up Mrs. Guire's small, trembling hand. "Ryan will be here in just a minute. He is at the clinic."

"It passes," said Patricia breathlessly.

"How long has this been going on?" Amber prayed the rumble she heard was Ryan's 1968 black Mustang starting. As rarely as she called him at the clinic, he would know this was an emergency.

"I don't know," said Patricia, beads of sweat forming on her forehead.

Ryan Griffin pulled up in front of the house and turned the car off. Grabbing a medical bag, he jumped out of the car, a lock of dark hair falling on his forehead. Running most mornings with Peter helped keep his twenty-five-year-old body in great shape, but his wavy hair resisted control. "What's up, ladies?"

Amber gave Mrs. Guire a moment to answer, but she barely acknowledged Ryan's presence. "I was on my way home and saw her sitting here," said Amber. "She's not really talking much and didn't say anything when I called you."

Ryan looked at his elder sister, eyebrows rising. Patricia Guire was not known around town for quiet compliance. He kneeled in front of the older woman and felt for a pulse in her wrist. "What are you feeling, Mrs. Guire?"

"Tired," said Patricia. "I'm just…tired."

"Uh-huh," said Ryan. "Anything else? Any pain?"

"I just need…to lie down." She shifted her eyes to look at Ryan for the first time since he arrived. "It passes."

"Does it now," said Ryan. "And how often does it pass?" Ryan

3

pulled out a pulse oximeter and attached it to Patricia's left index finger.

"Every few days or so." Patricia's voice was soft but becoming more steady.

Amber turned to look through her car window but didn't see any movement from the car seat. She prayed Daniel still slept peacefully.

"Are we talking more than once a week?" said Ryan as he watched the reading on the pulse ox machine.

"Not normally." Patricia's eyes were clearing, and she watched Ryan's movements.

"How about you let us help you inside so we can get this jacket off?" said Ryan. "I'd like to take your blood pressure."

"No need to worry," said Patricia, weakly waving him off. "If I can just rest for a while…"

"Mrs. Guire," said Ryan. "That wasn't really a request."

Amber watched the two of them size each other up. She'd never seen her brother stand up to Mrs. Guire quite like this before, but she knew his obstinate side very well. Just five years younger than she was, she remembered many stand-offs growing up.

After a brief moment, Patricia nodded. "Okay."

Ryan extended both his arms, and Mrs. Guire leaned on him heavily as she stood.

"I'm just going to grab Daniel from the car," said Amber.

"Oh, child," said Patricia, "go on home." Patricia carefully climbed a step, obviously relying on Ryan to steady her. "I'm fine. Really."

"With all due respect, Mrs. Guire," said Amber, "I'll feel much better once Ryan's convinced you're fine."

Amber opened the front door of her Jeep and turned the engine off, then went to the back door and opened it to see Daniel looking at her. "Hey there, handsome." She unlatched the seatbelt and pulled the car seat towards her. "We're just going to go inside Mrs. Guire's house for a few minutes."

By the time she made it inside, Ryan had Patricia sitting on her couch and was helping her out of her jacket. She seemed like a weak version of her normal self, yet more responsive than before.

"I don't know why you think this is necessary," said Patricia.

Ryan fastened the blood pressure cuff around her right arm. "Because you were sitting on your front porch allowing me to attach medical equipment to you without an argument."

"I simply over-exerted myself for a moment," said Patricia.

"Really," said Ryan calmly. "Doing what?" He inflated the blood pressure cuff.

"I was tending to my bluebells in the garden," said Patricia.

As he began to release the pressure on the cuff, he felt her pulse at her wrist again. "And what were you doing last time this happened?" asked Ryan.

"Last time?"

"Yes," said Ryan. "You said this happens once a week or more. Were you also tending the garden last time?"

"That's not any of your concern," snapped Patricia.

"It's good to hear your attitude returning to normal," said Ryan.

Amber felt the tension rising in the room but wasn't sure what to do to help.

"Now you listen to me, young man," Patricia began.

"No, ma'am," said Ryan. "You listen to me." He sat down on the couch beside her and removed the blood pressure cuff. "I don't know how often your family checks on you by phone, but with the exception of your niece's trip here six months ago, I've not seen any of them rumble into town."

"I dare say nothing rumbles in this town but that old Mustang of yours," Patricia muttered.

Ryan continued on without letting her distract him. "And

I'm willing to bet that I'm the closest thing to a doctor that you've seen in a long time."

Patricia crossed her arms. "What's that got to do with anything?"

"Mrs. Guire, as both a medical professional and a friend, I care about you. And what I saw when I first got here concerns me."

"Is my blood pressure bad?"

"It's not horrible," said Ryan.

"And that contraption you put on my finger. Was it reading okay?"

"It was acceptable."

"So what exactly are you proposing?"

"I'd like to start by testing your blood sugar now."

Patricia raised her eyebrows. "You think I'm diabetic, boy?"

"That's one possibility."

"And what are the other possibilities?"

"Truthfully, Mrs. Guire, the possibilities are quite extensive because I have a very short list of symptoms. I'd really like you to come back to the clinic to tell me more about what's been going on and to allow me to draw blood for some tests."

"And what if I don't want to?"

"I don't mind setting up shop right here. I have quite a bit of what I need in that bag." Ryan pointed his index finger in her face. "And I'm not above calling someone to bring me every-thing else so you don't have a chance to lock me out."

Patricia grabbed his finger. "You're about the most irritating boy in this whole town."

Ryan grinned at her. "I'll take that as a yes."

CHAPTER 2

*C*ONVINCED HER JEEP WAS EASIER for Patricia to get out of than Ryan's Mustang, Amber insisted on driving her to the clinic. Upon arriving at the front door, Patricia thanked her for the ride. Ryan opened her door and held his hands out to assist her. "I wouldn't get used to this, young man," she said as she leaned on him to get out of the Jeep.

Ryan shut the vehicle door and waved to his sister. "I'm rather counting on you hanging around for a while to help spoil Alaina."

"How old is your sweet child now?" Patricia knew she was moving more slowly than normal, but her steps were taking so much effort.

"Two weeks old today. We thought she and Peter might share a birthday, as late as she was coming."

Ryan opened the front door of the clinic, and Patricia shuffled through, pausing in the small waiting area. Two people sat in chairs to her right, and Patricia determined not to look to see who was going to know she'd come in the door on Ryan's arm.

"Hey, Becka," said Ryan. "Is Exam 2 open?"

Becka's blonde ponytail bounced with each movement of

her head. "Sure is," the receptionist replied before answering the ringing phone.

"Just a little farther, Mrs. Guire," said Ryan. "We're going back here to the left."

Patricia straightened her spine and gave each step concentrated effort. *I will not look like an invalid*, she thought.

Just as they reached the exam room door, the door to the right opened. Dr. John Williams stood to the side while seven-year-old Joshua Davis and his mother, Amy, stepped out.

"Hey, Doc Ryan!" said Josh. "Doc John says I'm doing great!" Josh emphasized his last word by jumping as high as he could with his fist in the air.

Patricia thought back three years when Ryan first appeared in Crossing, before the days that Crossing had a regular doctor in the clinic. Josh had been showing signs of a flu that wouldn't go away and nose bleeds every few days. When the small child had fainted at Amber's wedding reception, Ryan had been the one who insisted on taking the child straight to Doernbecher Children's Hospital in Portland, where he had been diagnosed with Acute Lymphoblastic Leukemia.

"Give me five," said Ryan, holding his hand out for the child to hit.

"C'mon, Josh," said Amy. "Let's not 'old everyone up."

Patricia smiled at Amy as she directed her child toward the front door; then her eyes briefly met Dr. Williams'. She jerked away, releasing Ryan's arm so she could walk into the exam room.

"Everything okay?" said Dr. Williams.

"Yeah," said Ryan. "Just doing some routine checks."

"Let me know if you need me," Patricia heard Dr. Williams say.

She refused to acknowledge his presence in the hallway. She could sense Ryan's confusion, and she knew she was being rude, but she would take a firm stance. She could not let her guard down.

Finally, the doctor moved on, and Ryan shut the door.

"Want to tell me what that was about?" said Ryan, walking over to help Patricia sit up on the exam table.

"I thought you wanted to hear more about my episodes."

"I do. I'm just wondering if whatever that was has anything to do with your episodes."

Patricia breathed in deeply and folded her hands in her lap. "He and I have a history I'd rather not repeat. That's all." She turned to focus intently on Ryan. "What are your other questions?"

Ryan watched her for a moment. "Interesting." He picked up a clipboard with papers attached and grabbed a pen. "Okay, let's talk about these episodes. When did they start?"

AMBER PULLED IN FRONT OF HER LOG CABIN HOME AND SIGHED deeply. The scene before her was calming. The young maple tree in the front yard was budding, small flowers were beginning to poke their heads out of the dirt in front of the long deck, and a soft glow was coming through the front windows. "Daddy's home, baby boy," she whispered.

Daniel had started whimpering before they dropped Patricia off at the clinic. Now he was fully upset. Between the doctor's office, the long drive, finding Patricia, and Daniel's cries from the back seat, her nerves were shot.

Just as she released Daniel's car seat and pulled it to her, Peter opened the front door. "Want some help, Ray?" Their Australian shepherd, Sassy, barked beside him.

"Yes." She smiled. She marveled at how Peter still calmed her. *Thanks, God, for bringing us together.*

She grabbed her purse and the diaper bag from the floorboard and then moved out of the way so Peter could get to Daniel. He easily lifted the car seat, closed the Jeep door, and wrapped his free arm around Amber while they walked inside. He adjusted his much longer stride to her shorter steps.

"I was starting to wonder about you two," said Peter.

Amber set the bags down beside the soft leather couch and turned to greet Sassy, who spent most of her time with Amber. "It's been quite a day," she said, rubbing the dog's dark brown ears.

Amber saw concern etched in Peter's blue eyes before he turned his focus to pulling Daniel from the car seat. "Everything go okay in Portland?" he said, patting the child's back.

Amber sighed as she adjusted a pillow on the couch behind her and prepared to nurse her baby. "Yeah, and I have a lot to tell you about that. We have some decisions to make. But on the way home, I found Patricia Guire on her porch steps."

"Her porch steps?"

Peter handed Daniel to Amber before sitting down beside her, and while the baby latched on and began to eat, Amber told Peter about how Patricia looked and calling Ryan.

"Did Ryan say what he thought was going on?"

"Can you grab me a rag or something?" Amber wiped the small stream of milk on Daniel's cheek. "He mentioned diabetes, but he said he had so little information that he had a long list of ideas. I took her to the clinic where she was going to talk with Ryan more and let him take some blood to send to the lab."

"Well, we know she's in good hands. Ryan will do his best."

Amber shifted slightly so she could lean into Peter. He wrapped one arm around her. "I know. I guess I'm just remembering how fragile life can be. I know in my head that none of us is promised tomorrow, but life just seems to go on, and I don't spend a lot of time thinking about someone not being there."

"That's quite a statement," said Peter.

"What do you mean?"

Daniel let go and turned his head to look at Peter. Amber wiped around his mouth and handed him off to Peter while she adjusted her clothing. Peter placed Daniel on his shoulder to pat his back.

"You spent six years in a family that was falling apart after the death of your sister, then ten years on the road running from the reality of that. For you to say that you don't spend a lot of time thinking about someone dying shows God has really done a lot of healing in the past three years."

"Maybe." Amber thought for a moment. "Or could it just be that I expect things to continue tomorrow as they were today?"

"Do you?"

Amber looked at her husband just as Daniel gave two small burps. She handed him the rag in case any milk came up with the burps.

"Or do you expect God to work and change things according to His plan?"

Amber sighed. "I pray for God's best. I know He'll take care of us and guide us. But I'm not sure I spend any time thinking about what that means, what that looks like in terms of tomorrow."

"All it means is that tomorrow could be different. The question you need to settle is if you're okay with that."

Amber sat quiet for a minute, her thoughts circling through different arguments in her head. Finally, she said, "I guess, if I truly want God's best and I really trust Him, then I have to be okay with whatever comes. I may be sad or I may not like it, but ultimately, I have to trust in God's love for me."

CHAPTER 3

*J*UST AFTER LUNCH THE NEXT afternoon, Amber knocked on the front door of Ryan and Brittney's one-story log cabin. Ryan, holding a sleeping two-week-old Alaina, opened the door. Amber could see Brittney on the edge of the overstuffed leather couch, tying her shoes.

"Please say you feel like going for a walk," Brittney said. Her long, auburn hair pulled back in a messy bun, her dark eyes pleaded with Amber for escape.

Amber laughed. "Sure. Feeling trapped?"

"Staying home sounds like such a luxury until you can't do anything but stay home!" said Brittney.

"Just take it easy, Britt," said Ryan. "Not too fast and don't go too far. Your body is still recovering from giving birth." Amber looked at Alaina, her dark hair spiking out in odd directions from the top of her head.

"Yes, doctor," said Brittney, rolling her eyes. "Come on, Amber, before he decides I need a wheelchair!"

Brittney gave her husband a quick kiss, and the girls headed out the door and towards a well-worn path beside the house. If they followed the path long enough, it would wind past Peter and Brittney's parents' home and eventually to Peter and Amber's home.

"Are you still feel pretty good?" said Amber.

"Yeah," said Brittney. "But then after almost forty-two full weeks of pregnancy, even the day after giving birth felt better!"

Amber looked up at the tall trees around her. Even though their feet crunched leaves on the ground from the past fall, the maples and oaks were all coming to life with the spring. She reached down to grab a small dead branch from the path.

"Tell me what happened at Daniel's doctor appointment yesterday. Mom said it went well, but she wasn't sure she had all the details right."

Amber sighed. "The physiological test on his ears still shows some abnormalities, which is why they did the tym-pan-nom-i-tree. Am I saying that right?"

"Pretty close," said Brittney, putting her hands in her pockets. "Tympanometry is where they test the eardrum, right? In all my nursing classes, I was always horrible at the ear, nose, and throat stuff."

"Yep, it tests how well the eardrum moves. And apparently Daniel's eardrums are great. The other test also came back good," said Amber, concentrating for a moment, "bone conduction test, I think. The one that tests the inner ear."

"So, now they know that the problem is definitely with his middle ears?"

Amber began peeling back a little of the loose bark on her stick. "Yes."

"What's next?"

Amber paused in the path and looked at the trees around her. Some of them reached 200 feet over her head.

"Britt, do you ever wonder why God chose to make the fir trees here so tall?" Amber focused for a moment on the variety of life around her. "Even the cedars and cottonwoods tower over the maples."

Brittney reached out and put her arm on Amber's shoulder. "What's that got to do with Daniel?"

Amber looked at the maple tree nearby, her eyes brimming with tears. "I feel so inadequate." She looked at Brittney, the tears beginning to overflow. "We have a beautiful baby boy. I know that. I should be thankful." Amber wiped away a tear running down her cheek, swallowing and trying to get some control over her emotions. "I'm thankful. I am. But everything the doctors talk about, sign language and hearing aids and directional microphones and... I just don't know if I can do this."

"Oh, girl," said Brittney, her eyes feeling with tears of empathy for her sister-in-law.

"Why did God give Daniel to us? Why not to you and Ryan? You guys are the ones with medical training. This would be so much easier for you."

"Maybe that's exactly why." Brittney grabbed both of Amber's hands and squeezed tight. "Because God knows that you will rely on Him to get you through this. Ryan and I would keep defaulting to our medical training and connections."

Brittney took one of her hands and motioned to all the trees around them. "All these grand and glorious trees. Each one unique and each one serves a great purpose, even the maple. Don't wish your purpose away just because another one looks easier."

Amber hugged Brittney tight. *God, help me*, she prayed.

THE NEXT WEDNESDAY, PATRICIA SAT IN A WHITE WICKER CAMEL back rocking chair on her front porch enjoying the sunshine and warmer temperatures. The afternoon was coming alive with children playing outside after school; she loved listening to the laughter and screams of delight.

Her mind was just beginning to wander back in time when a familiar rumble pulled in front of her house. Ryan stepped out of his Mustang and walked towards her.

"You ever gonna get that hair cut?"

Ryan leaned on the railing along the steps and smirked at her. "You don't like the curls?"

"They're better suited on a girl. I like that spikey style you wore over the winter."

Ryan laughed. "Yeah, well, to be honest, I do too. I'm heading to the barber shop after I talk with you."

"Get on with it, then. Guessing you got test results to give me."

Ryan sat in a wicker chair beside her, leaning forward with his elbows on his knees. "I do have results, and they are all looking good. You know your blood pressure is okay, and your blood sugar levels are within acceptable levels."

She leaned in, anxious for the bottom line.

"Your thyroid is fine, and your heart is great for a sixty-six-year old woman."

"If everything is so good, then what is causing the pain, Ryan?"

Ryan looked at her for a moment. "I think that's the first time you've called me by only my first name."

Patricia sat back and tried to dismiss the moment. "Don't go reading nuthin' into that."

Ryan leaned back in his chair, bringing one leg up to rest his ankle on his opposite knee. "Mrs. Guire, I don't think anything is seriously wrong with you."

Patricia looked at him, confused about the symptoms that had been plaguing her for months. "Then why the pain?"

Ryan sat quiet for a moment, like he was uncertain how to proceed.

"Spit it out, boy."

"I think you are having panic attacks."

"Panic attacks? Why on earth would I panic while tending my garden?"

"The symptoms all fit: sweating, trembling, shortness of breath, chest pain, dizziness. Even the tingling in your fingers. They usually last ten minutes or less and tend to take a toll on your body so you feel wiped out afterwards."

"But what would cause me to panic? That doesn't make any sense."

"Sometimes panic attacks start over real fears, life-and-death situations, or circumstances where we truly believe that we are in danger of some sort."

Patricia motioned toward her flower garden. "There is nothing dangerous in that garden."

She watched Ryan's jaw tighten. "Just because we believe we are in danger doesn't necessarily mean it's true."

Patricia thought about his statement for a moment. His facial expressions were masking something. "You sayin' that this is all in my head?"

"I'm just…"

"You listen to me, boy," said Patricia as she stood from her chair, "although I've accused you of it a time or two, I don't believe for one moment that you are dense." She pointed her finger in his face. "A bug or two in that garden hadn't ever sent me running before. So please tell me what exactly you think has got me all terrified without me knowin' it."

Ryan stood, forcing Patricia to take a step back. "Mrs. Guire, let me be clear. I don't think these panic attacks have anything to do with your garden."

"What then?"

"I'd like for you to trust me enough to tell me."

"What are you talking about?"

Ryan put his hands in his pockets and walked toward the porch railing. He took a deep breath and then turned to face her. "These panic attacks started about three years ago, about the time Dr. Williams came to town."

Ryan's words exploded in Patricia's head. *Dr. Williams! Could it be true? Is that what this is all about?* She turned and walked a couple steps away from Ryan.

"I know there's a history there, and whatever it is has caused you to disappear from anyplace he likes to go. You never come to lunch at the diner anymore. Robert at the General Store asked about you last month because he hasn't seen you much…"

She heard Ryan walk up behind her.

"And you slip in and out of church, coming in late, sitting near the back, and leaving before the final prayer is finished."

This cannot be happening. Patricia reached out to find the railing in front her, looking for some support before she fell to her knees. Weakness seemed to be taking over. *Lord, why? After all these years? I thought this was in the past.*

Ryan moved around in front of her, placing one hand on her upper arm. "Mrs. Guire?"

She swallowed, trying to regain control of her voice. Her eyes burned, and she feared tears would soon come. She had to get inside, figure this out. "Thank you, Ryan. I won't keep you further."

Patricia turned with as much dignity as she could muster and walked inside her house, closing the door behind her.

CHAPTER 4

"*R*YAN," SAID AMBER.

"Hmmm," said Ryan, turning his head to look at his sister.

"It's your turn, dude," said Peter.

Peter, Amber, Ryan, and Brittney sat around the dining table at Peter and Amber's home Friday evening, a card game of Spades half-played before them. Daniel sat in a jungle-themed exersaucer near Peter, happily bouncing and chewing on plastic keys while Alaina lay sleeping in a bouncer near Brittney.

"Sorry," said Ryan. "My mind just isn't into cards tonight."

"Really?" said Brittney sarcastically.

"What's up?" said Peter.

"Nothing I can talk about," said Ryan. "Just a difficult patient."

"Has to be Mrs. Guire," said Amber, grabbing her glass and walking to the open kitchen to get herself more iced tea.

"You know I can't say anything, Sis," said Ryan.

Amber took a sip of her tea and leaned against the black-engineered stone countertop closest to the table. "Well, how about this? As a friend, should I be concerned enough to check on her, see how she's doing?"

Ryan looked at his sister, thankful for the relationship God had restored between them. But he needed to proceed cautiously so he wouldn't damage his professional integrity. "As your brother, I would encourage you to check on any friend that you found largely unresponsive on her front porch within the last week or so."

Amber nodded. "Consider it done. I'll call her tomorrow and set up a time for us to have lunch next week." She walked back to the table. "Now, can we get back to cards? I think Britt and I can win this hand."

"Ooh!" said Brittney. "If your hand is that good, we got this!"

"You girls have to be bluffing," said Peter, looking at his cards.

SATURDAY MORNING, PATRICIA SAW THE BANK ON THE CORNER and made her left turn onto East Powell Boulevard in Portland, Oregon. She settled back, letting traffic flow around her 2008 Ford Escape. Although it would be good to see Jake and his kids again, she was in no hurry.

When she'd called him earlier in the week, he'd decided to take part of the day off from working in the garage they owned together so they could enjoy lunch. She'd missed her normal end-of-month appointment with him in April, and she could hear the concern in his voice.

She turned onto Southeast 62nd Avenue and soon saw his old Nissan Quest minivan beside the little white house. Seven-year-old Andrew sat on the front porch step, his blond hair almost sticking up more than it was lying down.

As soon as he saw her, he jumped up and ran inside. Before

she had the engine turned off, both he and five-year-old Emma were running toward her.

Andrew opened her door. "I thought you'd never get here!" He beamed at her, bouncing as he waited for her to get out of the vehicle.

"Well, here I am," said Patricia, grinning at the enthusiastic greeting.

"We've been waiting simply forever!" said Emma, one front tooth conspicuously missing in her smile. "But now you're here, and we can have fun!"

Patricia got out of the car and retrieved a bag from the back seat. "Were you not having fun before I got here?"

Emma crossed her arms. "No! We had to do chores—"

"All morning—" said Andrew.

"And they took forever—" said Emma.

"But Daddy said that when you got here—" said Andrew.

"We could play!" said Emma.

As they slowly made their way to the front door, Patricia dutifully listened as the children excitedly told her all the things they'd done that morning to prepare for her visit. Patricia looked up to see Jake and nine-year-old Taylor waiting for her on the front step.

Patricia took both hands and pushed Emma's light brown bangs from her eyes. Moving in close, Patricia said, "So now must be time for fun."

Emma's smile lit up her entire face.

"Me too!" said Andrew, jumping up and down.

"You too," said Patricia, smiling while she tousled his hair. "Presents for all!" she announced, holding up a large bag hanging off her arm.

Jake shook his balding head, grinning. "You spoil them."

"A grandmother's prerogative," she said seriously.

"One I won't deny you," said Jake, taking his arm from around Taylor's slight frame to give Patricia a hug. "I appreciate you stepping in to be a grandmother since their own are so distant."

"It is my pleasure," said Patricia as she touched Taylor's cheek. "Now, come inside, everyone, so I can sit down."

Jake held the door while Andrew and Emma rushed into the small living room and Taylor wrapped her arm around Patricia's waist to walk beside her.

"I see you have new glasses, child," said Patricia.

"Yeah, the other ones were getting old," said Taylor, pushing the small metal frames farther up her nose.

"I like the purple color," said Patricia. "It suits you."

Taylor smiled.

Patricia sat on a worn blue couch just inside the door, the large picture window behind her. Taylor sat beside her, and Andrew and Emma sat on the hardwood floor at her feet. Jake took a seat in a teal-colored chair on the adjacent wall. Patricia opened up her bag and pulled out the first box. "For my little Emma."

Patricia handed over a brightly wrapped box. Emma tore open the paper, pieces flying everywhere. She looked at the box, uncertain. She tried to sound out the words. "A – s – t – r – o..."

"Very good," said Patricia. "It says *astrolamp*. It shines stars on your wall at night."

Emma's eyes lit up. "My very own stars? In my very own room? Daddy!! Do you see? I simply can't wait! How long until dark?"

Her chatter faded slightly as Patricia pulled out another box. "For my Andrew."

He barely tore the paper off one side before he stopped and looked at the box. He jumped up, shouting, "Woo hoo!! A rocket! Yes! Look, Dad!"

"A rocket?" Jake looked suspiciously at Patricia as he took the box from his son.

"Just a stomp rocket," she defended herself. "I remembered

my promise after the science kit that I wouldn't bring anymore exploding or volcano-like substances into the house."

"Or things that stain," added Taylor. "It took Megan a week to get all that blue out of her hair."

"Megan?" said Patricia.

"A girl at school," said Taylor. "Somehow Andrew put the blue dye from that science kit into a cup of water without the teacher seeing. Then as they sat at their desks, he took Megan's braid and dipped it in the cup. She didn't know what he was doing until the tips of her hair were dyed blue."

"It was so cool," said Andrew. "Her hair soaked it up just like the celery stalk did when we put it in red water!"

"That was science class," said Jake sternly to his son.

Andrew quickly sat down, subdued for the moment. "Yes, Dad."

"No more dye for Andrew," said Patricia, winking at the boy. He smiled back at her. "Now, for my Taylor," she said, pulling out a small box from her bag.

Taylor carefully pulled at the paper until she came to a small jewelry box. She opened the box and gasped. "Oh, Nanna!" Inside was a small dolphin pendant with a matching silver chain. She pulled it out to put it around her neck. Fastened, the dolphin fell to where her heart was. Taylor put her hand over the dolphin and looked at Patricia. "I will treasure it. Thank you."

"Okay, you guys go play," said Jake, "and we'll have lunch in a little bit." Andrew and Emma ran outside to set up his new rocket, while Taylor picked up a book from the coffee table and headed to her bedroom. Jake looked closely at Patricia. "You're different with them."

"I don't know what you mean," she said, picking up pieces of wrapping paper near her.

"Uh-huh. So what happened last month?"

"Things were just busy."

"Really? Too busy to come see the kids?"

Patricia just nodded.

"Patricia, I've known you for almost nine years. You took a chance on me and Kelly, hiring me to help us get back on our feet after our families disowned us when we came to Christ. You stepped in for our moms when the kids came along, supporting Kelly as she adjusted to motherhood. And I don't know what I would have done without you two years ago when Kel lost her battle with cancer."

Jake adjusted his glasses. "You missed last month's appointment to go over the books from the garage. And you show up today looking worn out and tired."

Patricia sighed. She didn't want to drag her past out for anyone to see, but Jake was more like a son to her than anyone. "I've been having some..." She paused, looking for the right words. "...health challenges."

Jake sat forward in his chair. "What kind of challenges?"

"Nothing serious."

Jake raised his eyebrows at her.

"Truly," she said. "Ryan has run all kinds of tests, and he said everything is fine."

"Then what is it?"

Patricia took a deep breath. "He says I'm having panic attacks."

"Panic attacks? Why?"

"We don't know for sure."

Jake sat back and looked at her for a moment. "But you suspect."

Patricia looked at the empty fireplace across from her. How she longed for a child to come running into the room to change the subject. "Yes."

"What are you going to do about it?"

"Do?"

"As I understand it, panic attacks are about being afraid. So what are you going to do to deal with the fear?"

Patricia hesitated.

"Or are you going to continue to live with the attacks?" said Jake.

CHAPTER 5

*T*HE SUN WAS HAVING LITTLE success in breaking through the cloud cover Sunday morning as Patricia walked into Jake's kitchen. Taylor stood at the stove, cooking scrambled eggs. "That looks good, child."

"Thanks. I made a little extra in case you wanted some too," said Taylor, gently stirring the eggs into fluffy, yellow lumps.

After breakfast, the family piled into Jake's minivan for the short drive to Mars Hill Church. Jake found a parking spot on Southeast Taylor Street, and they walked two blocks to the church. Patricia looked appreciatively at the hundred-year-old stone building. The rounded front with towers on either side had earned it the nickname "The Castle" from its members.

Patricia always loved walking into the main building for services with its huge open space, second story balcony, and plastered walls. She took her seat on one of the curved, wooden pews just as the bell tower rang to start the service and a violin player rushed to take her place on stage with the small orchestra.

After getting the kids to their classes, Jake settled in beside Patricia during the first song, and soon Pastor Tim Smith welcomed everyone. As Patricia looked at the multitude around her, it was hard to believe that this church had only been meeting together for a little over a year. The lanky pastor on stage looked like a strong wind would blow him over, but apparently he had the fortitude and demeanor God wanted to lead this menagerie of people.

That man has to be about my age, she thought, *and lots of people here are Jake's age, but this young lady in front of us might still be in college. And her hair! Is that blue dye or a reflection from the stained glass windows?*

Patricia tried to focus on Pastor Mark Driscoll's sermon that came through video feed from Mars Hill Church in Seattle, Washington, but the mix of the crowd kept drawing her. She'd never felt completely comfortable with the progressive attitude of the city, preferring the quiet pace of Crossing. *Something's obviously drawing the liberal-minded people of the city to check things out, and what they are finding is keeping them coming back. God, You must be part of this.*

As Pastor Mark closed out in prayer, Pastor Tim stood again, asking people to consider Mark's words and make some decisions in their own lives. After communion was offered, the service closed out with three more songs. Pastor Tim led the congregation in a new arrangement of "Just as I Am," causing Patricia's thoughts to circle back to her current dilemma.

Do I want to offer myself to You just as I am? she wondered.

She noted the silence in her heart and soul.

"WOW, THAT SMELLS GOOD!" AMBER SAID AS PATRICIA OPENED her front door to her two days later.

"Good. Bring that child in here and get you some, then," said Patricia, reaching out to touch Daniel's cheek as he snuggled against Amber's shoulder.

Amber followed Patricia through the living room to the kitchen that seemed permanently stuck in the 1970s. The yellow counter-top matched the green and yellow tiled laminate flooring, and all of it just added age to the worn-looking cabinets. The coffee maker was probably the newest appliance in the room, and it had to be ten years old.

Shredded chicken in a pot on the stove gently bubbled, and when Patricia removed the lid, the barbeque aroma escaped, causing Amber's stomach to growl. Patricia turned off the gas fire under the pot and carried it to the table where she had two plates, buns, a bag of chips, and a pitcher of tea waiting.

"Would you like ice?"

"Just a little," said Amber.

The ladies sat, Amber holding Daniel in her lap, while they prayed over their meal. She sat him on the floor at her feet and handed him a toy from his bag while Patricia began to spoon shredded barbeque chicken onto a bun for her.

"Tell me more about what's going on with your little one," said Patricia. "I've not spoken to Faye in a couple weeks."

"Well, basically we'll do more testing as he continues to grow, but the doctors are talking about a range of treatments. One day he might be a candidate for surgery, but right now they want to focus on hearing aids."

"Hearing aids? For a baby?" Patricia cut her sandwich in half before picking up one part to eat.

"Yes. How long he wears them each day will depend on how well he tolerates them, but we could go so far as to buy directional microphones to help."

"What's that?"

Amber wiped a drop of barbeque from her fingers onto a napkin. "It's kinda like a lapel microphone that a speaker at a conference or large church would wear, but it would be directed to Daniel's hearing aids and help him hear us above all the other noises around us when we speak."

"You gonna do that?" Patricia opened the bag of chips and offered some to Amber.

"Not right now. Perhaps later, maybe when he starts school. Peter and I've been praying a lot and believe we should go with a combination of the hearing aids and sign language." Amber got up to reposition Daniel before he scooted himself under her chair.

"Always wanted to learn sign language."

"I'm not sure I do!" said Amber as she laughed. "I've never tried another language before, and right now it seems overwhelming."

"Do you learn it from a book, or what?"

"The doctor recommended a friend of his. She lives in Arizona and recently broke her leg, so she's stuck at home. She learned sign language as a child because one of her parents is deaf, and she's willing to meet with me over webcam to teach me."

"Sounds like God intervening."

"Definitely," said Amber. "I've already talked to her once, and she seems really sweet. I think she's going to be a huge sup-port to me while I adjust to all Daniel's going to require as he becomes more mobile."

Amber picked Daniel up and balanced him on one of her legs. She pinched off a small piece of the bun and offered it to him. He opened his mouth wide. "Did you have a good Memorial Day?" Amber asked as she wiped her finger on her napkin.

"It was quiet."

"Didn't you spend the weekend with Jake and the kids?"

Patricia poured herself some more tea. "I drove up Saturday morning and came back Sunday after church."

"Things are all good there?" Daniel reached out for more of what was left of Amber's sandwich.

"Yes. Their church is really growing."

"I've heard really good things about Mars Hill," said Amber.

Patricia was quiet for a moment. Something Jake had said before she'd left had stuck with her, and she wondered if she should mention it to Amber. Truthfully, she didn't know if she wanted to mention it to anyone. She grabbed her plate, used her napkin to wipe crumbs into the trash, and then walked to the sink.

"Jake told me about a new group he's starting. Redemption Group, he called it." She kept her back to Amber, uncertain she wanted to see her reaction.

"That sounds interesting."

She heard Amber moving around behind her, but she couldn't quite tell what Amber was doing.

"It's for people who've..." she paused, fumbling in her mind for the right word. She wasn't quite ready to voice out loud what had happened to her. "People who've been hurt." She turned on the faucet to rinse her plate.

Amber walked up beside her with her plate and glass. "It sounds like Jake is doing a great thing," she said softly.

Patricia nodded. "It's just once a week. I could drive."

Amber laid her hand gently on Patricia's arm. "Are you asking me to go with you?"

"You've been hurt. I've been...hurt. I'll call and clear it with Jake."

Amber reached over Patricia and turned off the water. "I'd be honored."

Patricia looked at Amber and saw the tears threatening to overflow in her eyes. Patricia swallowed the lump in her throat, willing her voice to work. "I'll call him tonight."

CHAPTER 6

*A*MBER SAT SIDEWAYS ON HER couch, her legs crossed in front of her, supporting her laptop.

Peter quietly closed Daniel's bedroom. "I think he's finally down for the night," he said. Sassy wagged her tail as Peter stepped over her to slouch beside Amber, stretching his legs out on the coffee table and laying his head on the cushions behind him. "What are you doing?"

"I'm looking up more information on this Redemption Group thing Mrs. Guire mentioned."

Peter looked at her. "You said you'd go with her without knowing what you were agreeing to?"

"She looked so lost, Pete." Amber shrugged. "She was reaching out. I think she was asking for help in the only way she knows. I couldn't say no."

"Okay, so what are you finding out?" Peter readjusted to a more comfortable position and closed his eyes.

"The website says that they are small groups that deal with abuse, addictions, and trials. Ummm..." Amber read quietly for a moment. "It says that the groups only meet for about ten weeks, that people in the group are dealing with a variety of issues, and…" Amber paused as the reality of what she was reading sunk into her heart.

Peter opened one eye, turning his head slightly to look at her.

"And what?" he said gently.

She avoided looking at him, busying herself with closing down the Internet and shutting the lid to her computer. Peter grabbed her wrist.

"Ray? The group meets for ten weeks, and what?"

Amber swallowed hard, still unable to look at her husband. The man who loved her. The man who knew the mess she had been when she arrived in Crossing. The man who still didn't know everything about her past.

She fingered the seam at the bottom of her jammie pants. "It said that each group member is supposed to share their story."

She waited. Part of her mind still fought to remember that Peter was her patient and loving husband, not the angry boyfriend she'd escaped from years ago. He wasn't the one who had hurt her. He wasn't the one who had abandoned her as damaged goods in front of a hospital.

She finally raised her eyes to see him watching her.

"Are you ready to do that?"

"I don't know," she whispered.

Peter sighed. "Ray, I've never asked for a lot of details about your past, and that might be a mistake. I don't know. But I do know this." Peter took her hand and held it between his two hands, pulling it close to his heart. "You are an incredible woman. An incredible woman who carries a huge load from the past."

Tears began to gather in Amber's eyes as she listened.

"The baggage you insist on toting around is unnecessary. This secret that you guard so carefully—it wouldn't change my opinion of you."

Amber searched his eyes, desperate for solid proof that what he said was truth. Her mind went in circles, arguing all sides for her more quickly than she could sort it out.

Peter gently pulled her to him, laying her against his chest and wrapping his arms around her. "I love you, Rachel Amber Yager. And I'm committed to loving you for the rest of my days."

He kissed the top of her head as tears rolled down her cheeks. Hope fought to retain life among the doubts and fears in her heart. *Maybe God is working to put me into the Redemption Group because I need it as much as Mrs. Guire does.*

AMBER SAT IN THE LOGGING OFFICE THE NEXT MORNING, SHAKING her head. Yet another set of numbers was added incorrectly. For the last hour, she'd buried herself in the log count reports from Peter's young apprentice, who was frequently distracted by a pretty girl. Or a squirrel climbing a tree. Or the wind.

The phone ringing beside her was a welcome distraction. Her cheery greeting was cut short by Mrs. Guire.

"Child, I spoke to Jake. He said they don't normally do these groups in the summer, but a ladies group is going to start in June."

Amber looked at the calendar beside her. *June! That's tomorrow!*

Mrs. Guire continued. "Jake only leads guys' groups, but he called whoever it is that he needed to get permission from, and they are going to let us participate. We need to be at this lady's house on Tuesday."

Tuesday. Amber's mind raced. *Can I do this? I don't think I can do this. I need to tell her I can't do this.*

"I'll pick you up at your house about quarter after five. She said she'll have some food so you don't need to eat before we leave."

Mrs. Guire spit out the information and got off the phone quickly. Amber didn't remember saying much more than hello. She just sat and stared at the receiver for a moment before hang-ing up.

"Lord, what I really want to do is run from this group. I don't want to think about my story, much less tell it to anyone else."

She left her desk to walk to the window overlooking the for-est. The trees blurred together as her thoughts turned to the last time she'd seen Martin, the man who always brought darkness to her dreams. That final night, he'd been drunk and pushed her out of the car at the emergency room doors before driving off. She'd been so battered that she'd wanted to fade away. No one would have missed her.

Or so she thought.

Why couldn't Mom and Dad have found me before I'd met him, God? I know you protected me from other things while I was on the road. Why not him? No, that's not fair.

Sassy nosed her hand, pulling her out of her daydream. Amber bent down and rubbed the dog's brown ears. "I was weak, Sass."

Sassy tilted her head to one side, her chocolate-colored eyes attentive.

"I should have walked out the first time it happened, but I didn't. I chose to stay. It's my own fault things ended up the way they did."

Sassy growled her response. Amber stopped rubbing and just looked into the dog's eyes for a moment.

The door opened, and Amber looked up.

"You two having a moment?" said Peter.

Amber stood and walked back to her desk. "I think she was arguing with me."

"Who was winning?"

Amber looked at Peter sharply, and he put his hands up

defensively. "Don't take it out on me! I've lost plenty of battles to that canine."

Sassy barked.

Peter walked over to Amber and put his arms around her. "In fact, as I remember, one of those losses was over who she was going to live with when I moved out of Mom and Dad's. An adorable brunette won the loyalties of my own dog very quickly."

Amber giggled at the memory of a very red-faced Peter running into his mom's kitchen looking for Sass. The dog had given her allegiance to Amber within days of Amber's appearance, regardless of the fact that she had spent her first five years of life being wholeheartedly loyal to Peter.

"She's a pretty smart dog," said Peter.

Amber laid her head on her husband's chest and looked at Sassy still sitting near the window. "Yeah," she sighed. "I know."

"Anything you want to talk with a human about?"

Amber didn't lift her head. "Patricia called. Redemption Group starts Tuesday night."

"That's fast!"

"Yeah." Amber left the shelter of Peter's arms to walk back to the window. "I feel like God cleared the way for this to happen, but that doesn't make me any more excited about going."

"Nervous about sharing your story?"

Amber crossed her arms, running her hands up and down between her elbows and shoulders like she was cold. "What's the point in telling other people about this? What's the point of admitting where you failed in your past? It's passed. It's over. You can't change anything."

Peter walked up behind her and turned her around. He used his index finger to gently pull her face up until she looked in his eyes. "James tells us to confess our sins to each other and pray for each other so that we can be healed. You may think that

34

whatever it is you are hiding from is over, but it affects you. And that means it affects us."

Amber closed her eyes. "I just want it to go away."

"Then you have to deal with it, my Ray. I know it may not look like anything good can come from it, and I'm not saying that talking about it won't be scary. But where it's at now is giving the enemy of your soul great control. Talking about it in a safe place, admitting to people who love you where you really are—that gives God control to make something good and beautiful out of it."

Peter released her chin and held her close. Amber lay against him, savoring his embrace. She took a deep breath.

"Okay," she said. "I'll go and do my best."

She felt Peter's arms tighten around her. "That's my girl."

CHAPTER 7

*A*MBER SAT IN THE PASSENGER seat of Patricia's red Ford Escape Tuesday night, reading out the directions to the lady's house. From the path they were following, Patricia figured she lived fairly close to Mars Hill Church.

They pulled up in front of a small, dark gray house. The shades were partially drawn so you couldn't see much inside the house, but Patricia could see through the glass screen door that the front door was open. Lights shown brightly, yet she hesitated. At least the pots of flowers beginning to bloom around the front of the house made it seem more inviting.

Amber breathed deeply and looked at her. "Are you ready?"

Patricia barely nodded her agreement before opening her door. She felt more like she was going to a funeral than to a small group of Christian women.

A petite woman with long blond hair met them, holding open the glass door for them. "You must be Jake's friends. Welcome! I'm so glad you came tonight."

Patricia stepped into the home and noticed the tasteful décor. The hallway leading to the kitchen and the quaint living room were pleasantly full of furniture without being overloaded. Three other ladies were standing, watching the newcomers and waiting expectantly.

"Well, I'm Shannon," said the blonde, "and this should be everyone. So why don't we get introductions out of the way, and then we can get some food."

Shannon walked closer to the group of ladies gathered in her living room. Patricia briefly studied each woman as Shannon introduced them, wondering about their reasons for coming. Tabitha's short, stringy brown hair and the dark circles under her eyes made her look much older than she probably was. Lynn reminded her of a middle-aged soccer mom who shouldn't have any major issues, but then Patricia reminded herself why she was here. And Debbie's eyes sparkled with so much life that Patricia wondered about the 100 pounds or so of extra weight. *Is she sick or on medication, or is the weight a symptom of something deeper?*

Shannon prayed over the food and then led the way into the kitchen. The counter overflowed with food and snacks much like Patricia was used to seeing at Faye's house. Maybe this wouldn't be so bad after all.

AMBER FINGERED THE BOOKS SHE HELD IN HER LAP THAT SHE'D received in the meeting, *Redemption* by Mike Wilkerson and *Rid of My Disgrace* by Justin and Lindsey Holcomb. Shannon told them that they would be using the books in the group as they walked through these next several weeks together.

Patricia was quiet in the seat beside her as they traveled back to Crossing. *We've both been quiet, and we're almost home.*

"What did you think?" Amber asked cautiously.

"I think that maybe I'm not as alone as I thought I was three hours ago," said Patricia.

"Shannon's story is amazing. I would have never guessed

how much she's been through based on the woman who met us at the door. I thought maybe she was a trained psychologist or something."

"Yes. She certainly appears to have it all together now."

"And she said her husband, Nick, has his own story," said Amber. She looked out her passenger window as Patricia pulled into Crossing. Amber hesitated to continue. "Do you...do you think that two people having both been through pain..." Amber paused, uncertain how to continue. "Do you think it makes marriage easier? Understanding where the other one has come from? Or maybe harder because the pain from their pasts keeps interfering?"

Patricia wasn't quick to answer. "Child, I've been around Frank and Faye most of my life, and as far as I can tell, neither one was touched by the pain you and I bear before the day they wed. But it doesn't mean difficulties never came."

Amber thought back to the child they'd lost and the struggle she knew it had been for Faye to come out of that. *Is that the struggle I'm now facing? Am I really struggling, trying to figure out if it's worth it?*

"No," said Patricia after a brief pause, "I don't think it has as much to do with pain as it has to do with the simple determination to finish what you started."

Amber considered that. Faye had certainly made a tremendous difference in her life, and in countless other lives all over Crossing. Learning from her pain of losing a child seemed to make her stronger. *No, I think I'm asking myself the wrong questions. If I look at the example Faye provides, then I know struggling through the pain is worth it. Maybe the better question is if I really want to do this. But I believe God set this up, so He wants me to do this. If I don't, I'd be disobeying. He's provided the support and He's giving me the tools...*

Patricia pulled in front of Amber's house. The front porch light was on even though the sun wasn't completely set. Her husband and son were waiting for her. Tears began to form, and she looked at Patricia.

"My mind is just going in circles. I think I need to do this, but I'm not sure I can."

Patricia nodded and reached out to grab Amber's hand. "Fight fear with truth. You are not alone in your fear; you are not alone in your pain. And neither fear nor pain is from God. He wants to free us both from what we carry."

Amber released her seat belt and stretched across the seats to give Patricia a hug. "Pray for me this week, and I will pray for you."

PATRICIA ENTERED HER HOME AND LOCKED THE DOOR BEHIND her. The evening had been more draining than she anticipated as she stretched beyond her comfort zone to attend the Redemption Group. "Hmm," she said, looking toward the ceiling. "I see Your hand all over this thing, God, but I'm with Amber. I'd rather sit at home next Tuesday."

Tired as she was, the brief information Shannon had shared about the books in her hand made her curious. She crossed to her favorite spot on the couch and wearily sat, putting her feet on a small stool.

She looked at the cover of *Redemption*. The focus was on a man's back, covered in scars. Darkness encroached from the left as he lay in what appeared to be desert sand. "Not much there," she muttered, but then she realized the landscape wasn't as barren as she first thought. In one corner she saw hills and cliffs. "Is that water in the distance?"

Afraid she might miss something important, she ignored the urge to start with chapter 1 and instead opened to the foreword penned by Pastor Mark Driscoll. The first words caught her attention. "I suffer, therefore I am." The story of the book drew her in, her imagination caught by the depth of care and concern she felt behind the words.

She made it about halfway through the introduction before she had to stop reading. Her mind churned at the magnitude of people represented in the statistics shared by Pastor Mark. "If this book is to be believed, then obviously I am not alone in my experience, but..."

Patricia stood and walked away from the couch, leaving the book sitting on the cushion. "I know You know everything, God, and that You are everywhere. But I've never before considered..." She paused, turning to look back at the book, thinking about what she'd just read. "Could You have been...were You *there?*"

Her mind raced back to the darkness in her past, the moments she'd so desperately tried to forget.

"If I really believe You are everywhere," she reasoned, "then I can't just believe that you know about it. I have to believe You were there."

Her mind continued to circle around, struggling to make sense of her thoughts. "But if You were there... No, You didn't condone it. But You must have allowed it. And if You allowed it, then either You didn't care or You couldn't stop it."

She walked back to the table beside the couch, gently touching her worn Bible. "No, I don't believe that. Your Bible tells me You care more than I can fathom, and You are Creator of everything. No, power is not the issue. I must not be seeing something. There must be a third option."

She waited, almost expecting an audible reply. After a moment she turned abruptly to go down the hall to her bedroom. "Ah!" she cried, waving her hand, dismissing the book. She took just a step or two before turning back. "Can You not answer me now?" she shouted at the ceiling. "Perhaps this is why I believe You are..."

Patricia caught herself. She looked back at the book sitting on the cushion. "It's true," she softly exclaimed. "The book is right. Part of me does believe You are indifferent. You could have stopped that man, but You did not. You allowed him to…"

She walked to the nearest chair and numbly sat down. "It's no wonder You sometimes get quiet on me."

Patricia thought about times in her life when she'd felt God hadn't cared. Each time was during a difficult period, and each time she could see where she had assigned indifference to God's response to her. She shook her head. "Well, it's long past time to change that."

She stood, feeling the resolution to her core. "God, I believe you care and always have. I don't quite know how to change my thinking on the past, but I'm guessing You and I can figure that out a bit at a time."

She walked over and picked up *Redemption*, laying it gently on top of her Bible where she would see it early in the morning. "Tomorrow we're going to Genesis to read about Joseph. This book says he persevered because he saw Your plan, so I'm going to look at his story with Your help to see what I think. Seems I've got some learnin' to do."

Patricia turned and started to her room. "May I be a good student," she said, flipping off the light.

CHAPTER 8

*A*MBER COULD NO LONGER CONTROL the tears. She'd made herself comfortable on her couch Friday afternoon while Peter and Daniel headed to Crossing to pick up more saw blades for the wood shop. Skimming through *Redemption* had certainly given her some things to think about, but the second book Shannon had given her was the one that seemed to call to her. Now the book sat in her lap as she covered her face and sobbed.

Sassy sat up from her place on the floor and whimpered. Amber barely felt the dog lay her snout across her knee as she continued to release years of pain. Years of heartache. Years of loneliness.

She felt strong arms surround her and draw her close. Subconsciously, she knew it was Peter, but the tears would not stop. She leaned into him, grabbing his shirt like a lifeline. He gently rubbed her hair and held her.

Slowly, her pain subsided and the tears ceased. Peter offered her the box of tissues from the end table. She took it, lying exhausted against him.

"Want to tell me about it?"

Slowly, her weeks with Martin came out. She shared with Peter how attentive Martin had been in the beginning, how concerned he had seemed for her welfare. Until the day she'd burned dinner. Of course, he'd been remorseful afterwards. Mostly. The mess was still hers to clean up, but otherwise he'd been kind again. Until the next time.

Amber sat more upright on the couch, pulling her legs up in front of her. "When I first came to Crossing, I had all these negative thoughts and feelings about God. I felt like He'd let my sister die in the car accident when I was little and let my family fall apart. But meeting you and finding out that you too had lost a sister made me look at things with fresh eyes. I was able to reassign the blame of everything to the proper people."

Peter placed his arm along the back of the couch, rubbing a circular pattern on her shoulders. "Assigning blame to the right people is always a good step in the healing process," he said.

"I always believed Martin when he told me that it was my fault. And I placed more blame on myself for staying and taking it. Even after working things out over my sister's death, I still held that part of my life separate."

Amber took a deep breath, trusting the process she knew God had started in her. "I thought that God had abandoned me during that time because I was so dumb. I thought Jesus couldn't possibly understand all I went through." She turned and looked at Peter. "And I thought you wouldn't love me if you knew the mess I had been then."

"Oh, my Ray." Peter leaned forward and looked into her eyes. He grabbed both her hands and held tight. "I hope you know that my love is not based on anything you do or have done."

Amber's eyes burned. She'd shed so many tears that she didn't think more were possible, but the tenderness she saw in Peter's eyes overwhelmed her with gratitude.

"I do," she told him. She snuggled up against him. "And I know God cares, and I know Jesus understands. The book was just reminding me where it says in Hebrews that we have a great High Priest who can sympathize with our weaknesses. I remembered all Jesus went through on His journey to the cross. He was beaten and deserted. He knew exactly how I was feeling during those days with Martin."

Amber pushed a lock of hair behind her ear. "And before that He spent three years training and loving Judas. He knows exactly what it feels like to be betrayed by someone who claims to love you."

Peter kissed the top of her head. "Sounds like you are learning a lot."

"Yeah. I'm kinda looking forward to next Tuesday now. I know I've still got some hard work to do, but I feel so free, Peter. I'm not burdened with the secret of those days anymore."

"How about we celebrate? Dinner at Mom's?" He grinned at her.

Amber laughed and sat up to face him. "Is that where you left Daniel?"

Peter feigned innocence. "When I picked up the blades from the hardware store, Micah asked me to return some dishes to Mom that she had sent home with him last week full of leftovers."

"Mm, hmm," said Amber.

"When I stopped there, she was making her strawberry and angel food cake thing in that big punch bowl of hers, and of course it's way too much for her and Dad..."

"Of course," said Amber, smiling at the obvious ploy by her husband to get some of his favorite dessert.

"And, well, she offered to watch Daniel while I came home to see if you wanted to join them for dinner..."

Amber laughed. "Let me go wash my face and get shoes on, strawberry boy."

❄

PATRICIA DECIDED TO TAKE A WALK SATURDAY AFTERNOON. *Perhaps the fresh air will clear my head*, she thought. The morning had been pleasant enough, and she'd even picked up *Redemption* again. But the question she'd read right before slamming it shut still consumed her thoughts.

She tried to focus on the flowers hanging in baskets from her neighbors' front porches, the yards that could use a fresh trim, or the people working outside that she could wave to as she passed by, but the question continued to follow her. *To be without hope entirely, or to see hope and have it go away? Which is worse?*

She'd most certainly seen hope and watched it walk away.

Are you sure?

She stopped on the sidewalk at the sound of the quiet voice.

Did it walk away? Or did you walk away from it? the voice continued.

Her temper flared as she defended herself against the ludicrous suggestion. *Of course I walked away, she thought, but not like you make it sound. I...*

Her eyes saw the gray head of Dr. John Williams working in the garden beside his brother's house. John had retired from his big city job at Doernbecher Children's Hospital in Portland, and now he worked as the town doctor in the local clinic. She still didn't know the full story behind his sudden departure from what she imagined was a fancy life in the city to his brother's humble abode in a small town.

"I was protecting him," she whispered.

Tears filled her eyes, and she turned abruptly on her heel, determined not to walk close enough that he might greet her. The quiet voice was silent on her short walk back home, but the argument continued in her head.

I was protecting him. I was, she insisted as she stormed up her front porch steps. *He was busy with clinics and patients and networking with the other doctors. He didn't have time to worry about me or...*

About you or..., the quiet voice prompted.

A tear made its way down Patricia's cheek. She looked toward her garden, taking in the Mediterranean pink heath that covered the corner and headed around the house. That evergreen plant was precious to her, but few knew why she cared more for it than any other plant there. Only her sister understood.

Instead of going inside, Patricia sat in one of her rockers. She leaned her head against the back of the chair and sighed deeply. *If I'd known then where I'd be today, would I have done anything differently?*

"Is that the right question?"

The voice startled her, not much louder but certainly more forceful than the quiet one that had been speaking to her on her walk. She sat up in her chair and found herself looking into the bluest eyes she'd ever seen. His blonde hair blew gently in the breeze as he leaned comfortably against the porch railing, his blue jean clad legs crossed at the ankles.

She'd heard the stories of angelic visits in this town but never expected to receive one herself. "Matthew?" she said cautiously.

He simply nodded his head. "You're asking the wrong question."

Patricia struggled to remember what she'd been thinking about as she watched a western bluebird fly in and land on the railing near Matthew's hand. The bird's small blue head cocked slightly to one side as she hopped closer to him. He gently held out his hand, and the bird fluttered into it as a second bluebird landed on the railing.

"What is the right question?" Patricia asked.

"You are a great one for thinking yourself in circles, considering every possible angle and everyone's feelings."

"Isn't that what I should be doing?"

"Not always at the expense of yourself. And never at the expense of God's plan."

The bluebird chirped, turning her tiny black eyes to look at Patricia. She puffed up the muted blue and orange feathers on her breast and flapped her wings, flying over to sit on the railing near Patricia.

"She must be trusted with the knowledge. She must be given a choice to love in truth, or else it is not full love."

The reality of what Matthew was saying hit Patricia with blunt force. She couldn't take in a full breath. She felt herself trembling but knew she didn't have the strength to stand. Her chest hurt as she tried in vain to reach out for help.

A rumble echoed in her ears. She knew Ryan's Mustang was close, but would he stop? He'd said he'd check on her this week, but it was Saturday. He didn't work at the clinic on the weekends.

She tried to breathe calmly, but the pain swelled, and she settled for shallow breaths. She felt like she was burning up with fever. She started to look toward a sound in her driveway, but the movement made her head heavy. It felt like she was suddenly on a carnival ride as the earth rolled around her.

"Mrs. Guire?"

Ryan's voice. *Thank you, Lord!*

"Mrs. Guire, can you hear me?"

"I'll get the bag."

Was that Brittney with him? "I hear you." The words were a struggle, but she had to relieve the concern in his eyes.

"You keep talking to me, old woman, or I'll call an ambulance on you."

Brittney appeared within her sight, carrying a medical bag. She handed Ryan the blood pressure cuff and then pulled out the pulse oximeter and attached it to Patricia's index finger.

"Tell me what's going on, Mrs. Guire," said Ryan.

"Pain."

"Chest pain?"

"Yes. I'm a bit dizzy. And hot."

"Does it feel like the world is spinning?" said Ryan.

"A little. It's getting better."

Ryan looked at the blood pressure reading and then back at Patricia. "Are you going to tell me you were tending to your bluebells again?"

Patricia's head was clearing more, and the pain was subsiding. She wasn't quite ready to take a deep breath, but she cautiously turned to look at Ryan.

"No," she said. She paused, hesitant to continue. "I was talking to Matthew."

Brittney sat back on her heels. "Wasn't expecting that one."

Ryan's right eyebrow went up slightly. "Talking to Matthew about what exactly?"

Patricia took the deepest breath she dared. She lifted her jaw just a tad before blurting out, "About my daughter, Heather."

CHAPTER 9

*B*RITTNEY CAME BACK OUTSIDE WITH a glass of water and gently steadied it while Patricia drank a little. Ryan watched Patricia lean her head against the rocker.

"I planted that pink heath down there the very first spring I lived here," said Patricia. "My Heather was just about to turn one, and I wanted something to remember her, something close to me that wouldn't go away."

Brittney sat in the rocker beside Patricia, leaning in close with her elbows on her knees. "I never knew you had a daughter."

Patricia just nodded. "Not many do. Over the years, I would tend to that bush and pray for her, hoping she was happy. But I never spoke of her to anyone."

Ryan's mind processed the possibilities of this revelation, wondering if Heather had died. He removed the pulse oximeter from her finger, winding up the cord neatly as he cautiously asked, "What happened?"

Patricia hesitated, and Ryan watched her for signs of another panic attack developing as tears gathered in her eyes.

"She was adopted. At birth, straight from the hospital." A tear fell down each cheek. "I never felt as alone as I did that day," she whispered.

"How old were you?" said Brittney quietly.

Patricia wiped the tears from her cheek, pausing with her hands on her face. "Forty-one."

The age surprised Ryan. *Forty-one! This was no teenage discrepancy. What is going on?*

Patricia took a deep breath and began to stand. Ryan reached out to help her. He didn't want to be dealing with a broken hip or sprained ankle on top of the panic attacks.

"I'm tired," said Patricia. "I think I'll go lie down."

"Do you need any help?" said Brittney.

Patricia laid her hand on the side of Brittney's face and looked into her eyes. Ryan watched the tender moment, concern for Patricia growing inside him.

"I'll be fine," said Patricia. She reached out and grabbed Ryan's hand. "You're a good man, Ryan Griffin." After squeezing his hand gently, she quietly walked into her house and shut the door.

PATRICIA CLOSED THE FRONT DOOR AND SIGHED DEEPLY. *HEATHER. Her birthday is coming up again, just next week. This year she will be twenty-four.*

Twenty-four years since she handed over her baby and walked away. Not completely, but far enough. She had little right to speak into her life, much less tell her the truth as Matthew suggested.

But could I have done any different then? I was in no condition to handle a baby.

Her eyes fell to the book from the Redemption Group on the end table. Words she'd read earlier circulated in her mind.

Redemption is not about comfort. Initially, it may bring more pain. Well, at least they are honest.

Patricia padded down the hallway to her room. *What business does an old woman like me have in trying to fix decisions from my past? I've made my choices. Why can I not just live with them?*

She stopped in front of her dresser mirror and looked at the few family pictures that hung there. Her sister's gray eyes stared back at her, her silver hair perfectly in place. She shook her head. *I can't do it, God. Doing what Matthew suggested is going to mess up a lot of lives. Lives that went out of their way to help me when I most needed it.*

She waited, expecting an answer but not really wanting to hear what God thought about her decision. Nothing but silence came to her ears.

Rebellion. That's what it really is, she thought, disgusted with herself. *And that always worked out so well for the Israelites.* Her eyes went back to the picture of her sister.

"Ahh," she said, waving a dismissing hand at her reflection in the mirror. "I'm too tired to think about it." And she went to her bed to lie down.

The following Wednesday, Amber sat in her favorite over-sized chair at Peter's parents' house. She and his mom, Faye, had enjoyed lunch, during which Daniel had fallen asleep. Instead of disturbing him, she'd simply grabbed a book and settled in to read while Faye took care of some chores.

As she read, she came to a line that made her laugh. Realizing someone was walking by, she looked up a little self-consciously. Faye stood before her, smiling and holding an overflowing bas-ket of clean towels.

"Good book?" said Faye.

"It's one of the books we got from our Redemption Group," said Amber. "It's called *Rid of My Disgrace*."

Faye placed the basket on the couch. She pulled out a towel from the pile and began folding.

Amber continued. "I was just reading about identity, how we often identify ourselves within the boundaries of what has happened to us instead of who we really are. The authors quoted Lewis Smedes, who was a seminary professor. He said, "What I need is a sense that God accepts me, owns me, holds me, affirms me, and will never let me go even if he is not too impressed with what he has on his hands.""

Faye laughed. "That is quite a statement." Faye shook her head as she muttered to herself, "'Not too impressed with what he has on his hands.' Ain't that the truth."

Amber reached over to pick a towel from the basket. She sat quietly for a moment as she folded it, finally deciding to be brave and ask the question on her mind. "Have you ever struggled with your identity?"

"Oh, sure. I'd be willing to bet everyone does at some point in their lives. Probably more than once." Faye stopped in the middle of folding, hugging the towel in her hands as she looked into the distance. "I remember struggling a lot after the kids were born. Logan was quite an interruption into our lives at first, and I couldn't figure out how to be both a wife and a mother. I still loved Frank very much, but that child flat refused to stay on any kind of schedule. He always had to do things his way, and it seemed like I was always exhausted trying to keep up."

Faye began folding the towel in her arms again. "And Jamie coming along just barely two years later. I felt like I was just beginning to really figure things out, balance things between my husband and my child, and then I had to start all over again, figuring out how it all worked with a second child in the picture. I knew I was a wife, and I knew I was a mother, but I wasn't sure how to be both and whether that meant I lost me in the process."

"I remember one time," said Amber, "I was working as a waitress in a small diner, and this other waitress and I were talking. She told me that I had to love myself before I could love other people. But I didn't know how to do that. And repeating silly phrases like 'I'm loveable' just seemed to make me feel worse because I didn't really believe it."

"What did you think of yourself?"

"I thought that I was worthless, damaged." Amber took a deep breath. She arranged the towel on her lap and straightened out the edges, giving her fingers something to do. "I felt like I had nothing to offer anyone, nothing valuable that would cause anyone to care about me."

Faye sat down on the couch nearest Amber. "And now?"

Amber sighed, her eyes still focused on the towel in her lap. "I know those are lies. I know that there is no truth in them." She looked at Faye. "But I'm still working on replacing them with truth."

Faye reached out towards Amber. "Oh, my dear one."

Amber gave Faye her best attempt at a smile. "Most of the time I know I have value, but I also know that you and Peter and the rest of the family see more value in me than I see in myself."

Faye nodded. "Yes, I can understand that. I want you to hear me." Faye leaned in closer and grabbed Amber's hand. "The truth is that you were made in the image of God. He planned you and wants an abundant life for you. You are His treasured posses-sion, and He takes great pleasure in you. The rest of us get the great blessing of loving you."

Amber felt tears gathering as Faye spoke. She couldn't quite stand the intensity of love and truth she felt coming from her sweet mother-in-law, even though she desperately wanted to believe everything the woman said.

"Those are all promises from the Bible, dear one," said Faye. "Promises I once struggled to believe myself. I can write down where to find them if you want."

Amber let cleansing tears overflow. "Yes, please. I have a feeling that I will need to read them a lot in the coming days."

CHAPTER 10

ATRICIA GUIRE WAS NOT ONE Amber would ever label as chatty, but she'd been particularly quiet on the drive to Portland for their third meeting with the Redemption Group. She hadn't said much of anything during the session, and she hadn't said anything yet on the drive home.

"What did you think about tonight?" said Amber.

"It was fine," said Patricia.

"Did you imagine that Lynn was going through all that she shared tonight? She looks so…normal."

"Like you and me."

"Hmmm," said Amber. "I suppose so." She looked at Patricia. "I guess you never know what someone is hiding."

Patricia just looked at the road ahead.

Amber turned her head to look out her side window. "Sometimes I think I'm making great progress in sharing things from my past with Peter. And then he'll do something or say something that reminds me of another incident. Sometimes I'm hurt and sometimes I'm angry, but it's not really him, so I have to apologize and tell him more. It's all very draining."

"Then why do it?"

"What?"

Amber turned back to Patricia in time to see her purse her lips, and she wondered if she'd meant to say the words aloud.

"Did you ask me why I'm sharing all this with Peter?" said Amber.

"Well, if you feel you aren't making progress, then what's the point?"

"I don't think it's that I'm not making progress…"

"Surely some of what you tell him hurts him as well."

"Yes, some of what I tell him does cause him pain, but not because I'm striking out at him. He hurts because I hurt. But everything I share with him makes the pain less."

"His pain?" said Patricia. "Or your pain?"

Amber felt like Patricia had just reached out and slapped her. "Are you saying I'm hurting Peter—for no reason? That I should quit telling him what happened to me?"

"It's just something to consider," said Patricia quietly.

"I won't!" said Amber, crossing her arms. "I will not consider it for one moment! Clearly, holding everything in was not working. I couldn't get past my own failures, which meant part of me always defaulted to my old ways of thinking. Part of me doubted Peter's love for me and how long it would last."

Amber stopped for a moment trying to regain some control from her outburst. She stared out her passenger window, taking deep, slow breaths. *She's full of pain and doubts too*, she thought.

She tucked a lock of hair behind her ear. She cleared her throat and determined to speak calmly. "I dream of a full life with Peter, my heart yearns for that. But that's never going to happen as long as I withhold part of myself from him."

Patricia turned off the highway toward Crossing while Amber sat quietly in the passenger seat, waiting for some kind of response. After a few moments, she sighed. "Look, Mrs. Guire. You are the one who started this. You are the one who told me that God wanted to free us from our pain. Do you still believe that?"

Amber looked at Patricia. Both sat silently, and Amber hoped Patricia would say something.

Finally, she gave a gentle shake of her head. "I don't know what I think."

"When I first got here, Peter believed that facing my parents was the best thing. I held firm to his belief, and God brought us through it. Now it's my turn to be that anchor for you. Let me believe for both of us right now that God wants us to have an abundant life, free from our past and the pain it represents."

Patricia remained quiet as she turned down the road leading to Amber's home. She stopped in front of the house but still said nothing.

Amber reached over and grabbed her hand. "Please, Mrs. Guire. Don't let fear win."

Patricia looked at her hand in Amber's. "You don't know what I fear."

"No, I don't," said Amber. "But we serve a big God, and He not only knows the fear, He loves us very much."

Patricia said nothing.

"What is that verse about God not giving us a spirit of fear?" said Amber.

"First Timothy 1:7, child," Patricia said as she sighed. *"For the Spirit God gave us does not make us timid, but gives us power, love and self-discipline."*

For the first time, Patricia looked at Amber. She squeezed her hand gently. "I don't know that I can do what God asks."

"Three weeks ago, neither did I," said Amber. "And perhaps tomorrow you'll be the strong one and I'll be leaning on you for the faith I need to keep moving forward. But tonight, let me help you."

The battle going on in Patricia's mind was apparent by her expression. Finally, she conceded. "All right."

Amber smiled. "Good. Can I pray for you right now?"

Patricia nodded.

Without letting go of Patricia's hand, Amber bowed her head. "God, I just want to thank you for my friend ..."

AMBER WALKED INTO HER SOFTLY LIT HOME. MUSIC PLAYED IN the background as Peter lay on the couch, Daniel snoring on top of him. Sassy greeted her near the door.

Amber knelt down to rub the dog's ears. "I see you have things well under control here, girl," she said quietly.

"I get no credit?" Peter opened one eye.

Amber giggled. "Just resting your eyes, my sweet?"

"No sense in wasting a good opportunity."

Amber gently picked up Daniel and cuddled him close as Peter sat up on the couch.

"He was having trouble going to sleep tonight," said Peter. "Not sure what the problem was, but he didn't settle as easily as normal."

"Could be another tooth. His gum looked a bit inflamed this afternoon."

"Did you have a good meeting tonight?"

"Yeah," said Amber. "I'll go lay him down and tell you all about it."

While Amber settled Daniel in his crib, Peter made some of her favorite hot chocolate and lit lavender citronella candles on the front porch. They sat comfortably on padded deck chairs positioned just a few inches from each other and watched the stars.

"I've really been thinking a lot about Psalm 56," said Amber.

"Why that one in particular?"

"Well, it talks about God keeping track of our tears. I realized that if God was keeping track of my tears, then He must have seen them, and if He saw them, then He never once abandoned me. He always watched over me."

Peter watched her face. "That would mean He was there throughout your pain."

Amber looked at the stars and considered this for a moment. "Yes, and that's where it gets a bit muddled."

"What do you mean?" said Peter as he reached out for her hand.

Amber laced her fingers through his as she watched the stars overhead. "I know God didn't cause the pain. Martin has to bear responsibility for his choices, as I have to for mine. But He did allow it. Then I start to circle back with trying to reconcile a loving God and Him allowing evil."

"Where does that take you?"

"Right back to my sister dying." Amber look at Peter. "If I'm honest, all of this leads back to Cassie dying in the car accident that New Year's Eve. It was the catalyst that led to Dad's drinking and losing his job, us moving in with Mom's parents and Mom and Dad fighting all the time, and me running away and eventually ending up with Martin."

"True. But God preventing the car accident doesn't necessarily mean you would have been spared the pain of Martin or any of the other stuff. If the enemy of your soul wanted to attack you in that manner, Martin just happened to be in the right place at the right time to be the enemy's willing weapon of choice."

Amber looked back at the stars. "Maybe more of this stems from my belief in the purpose of pain and the ability of God. What do I really believe about God? Is He all-powerful? And just because He doesn't stop bad things, does that mean He isn't loving and good? Or could He see a greater purpose that will only come forth after pain that our enemy likes to inflict?"

"Surely I spoke of things I did not understand," said Peter.

Amber turned her head to look at him. "What?"

"It's what Job says near the end of his book. After he questions God about the calamity in his life, God answers with a series of questions like, 'Do you give the horse its strength?' All of them are pretty easy for Job to answer, but the one that always gets to me is when God asks if Job would discredit God's justice."

Amber sighed, looking at her hand intertwined in Peter's. "All of this just seems to come back to trusting God. Do I really trust Him or not? Could He possibly work something good out of all of this, or not?"

Peter gently pulled on her arm, guiding her out of her chair and over to his lap. He wrapped his arms around her. "And?"

"I don't know what good will come from it, but for tonight, at least, I believe He is working something out in me. I do trust Him." Amber looked into her husband's eyes. "How could I look at you and remember the last couple of years and not believe that He is good?"

CHAPTER 11

PATRICIA SLAMMED THE REDEMPTION book shut, very frustrated. Her anger seethed forth. "And what exactly am I supposed to do with that?" she yelled at her living room ceiling.

She walked to her front window and looked out at the cloudy morning. The street was quiet, even for a Thursday morning. School had been out for nearly a week, yet no children were outside playing right now. The scene outside seemed to echo her mood.

Thinking about the chapter she'd just read, she shook her head in irritation. "You send me to this blasted group, you partner me with this..." Patricia paused in her tirade.

She pictured Amber as she had seen her two nights ago in Shannon's living room during the group session. "Fine. She is changing, coming out from her pain. This is good for her."

"But that!" Patricia motioned back toward the book with a wave of her hand and looked back at her ceiling. "What am I supposed to do with that?"

"Forgiveness," she muttered. "I am not the one who needs to seek Your forgiveness! I did nothing wrong!"

She crossed her arms and looked out the window.

Are you certain? came the gentle reply.

"Certain? Certain!" Patricia spun around like she was talking to a physical person in the room. "*He* is the one who took everything from me. Everything! He trapped me and forced himself upon me and then just left me there. I didn't do anything wrong! I didn't even have an abortion. I did my best to care for that child, and when she was born, I made sure she had a good home."

Patricia allowed herself to think back on those months, the emotional turmoil she'd fought through to give her Heather a chance at life. "And I did it alone!" she shouted, her finger pointed in the air.

You were never meant to carry that burden alone.

The gentle words stopped her, the anger instantly gone. Her memories turned to John Williams, the adorable doctor who was painfully shy with his emotions. The quiet man who cautiously but consistently sought her out at her garage in Portland. He'd spent so much money on parts and services for his car before he'd found the nerve to ask her to dinner.

"But, I couldn't…" Patricia's eyes filled with tears, and her hands trembled. She walked back to her couch and sat. "I couldn't tell him."

Shame.

"Yes, I was so ashamed."

Fear.

"What if he didn't believe me?"

What if he had?

The dreams of the life she had given up overwhelmed Patricia. And, for the first time in many years, she gave in to the tears.

FROM NOON UNTIL THREE IN THE AFTERNOON DARKNESS CAME OVER all the land. About three in the afternoon Jesus cried out in a loud voice, "Eli, Eli, lema sabachthani?" (which means, "My God, my God, why have you forsaken me?").

Amber leaned over her desk at the logging office so completely absorbed in reading her Bible that she didn't hear the door open.

"Another good book, huh?" asked Faye, closing the door behind her.

"Hmm?" It took Amber a moment to refocus from what she'd been reading. "Oh, yeah," she said, smiling at Faye. "Just some things I'd never thought about before."

Faye handed Amber a foil-wrapped plate. "A new recipe, and I wanted your opinion."

Amber breathed deeply. "Smells like lemon." She pulled back the foil to reveal a yellow-colored cake with a smooth topping.

"Creamy lemon cake. Pretty easy, but a little time-consuming. I was thinking about making it for the family party over the fourth of July." She took a seat beside Amber's desk.

Amber took a generous bite. "Oh, wow." She savored the slight tartness and the velvety frosting before swallowing. "Pops is gonna love this!"

"Peter's grandfather has always liked lemon about as much as Peter likes strawberries."

Amber smiled as she leaned back in her chair. "And both of them give you a good excuse to bake."

Faye returned the smile, sitting in the chair near Amber's desk. "So, what were you reading?"

Amber swallowed another small bite and licked her lips. "I was reading Matthew's account of the crucifixion. Can you imagine God's distress when Jesus cried out, 'Why have you forsaken me?'"

"I've sometimes imagined Mary's response, or even the disciples. I can almost picture it. The heartbreak and disappointment. The confusion over what to do next. It must have been quite a crisis for them." Faye leaned back in the chair. "Hmmm. But God? I imagine Him focusing forward. I think He would have had to so He could stick with the plan."

"Both God and Jesus would have gone forward throughout history knowing the cross was coming. But the heart-breaking moment of truth was upon them."

"But just three days later," said Faye, "they stood in victory."

"Exactly!" said Amber, pointing her fork at Faye. "That's where I'm headed."

Faye looked confused. "I don't follow."

"God laid it all on the line, gave Jesus full control of the plan. And it was costly, and it hurt. Oh, I'm not explaining this well." Amber sat up in her chair. "It all goes back to that verse in… Hebrews, is it? The one that talks about us having a High Priest who understands?"

"Yes, Hebrews chapter 4, I believe."

"Because of the cross, God understands physical pain and emotional pain. He gets betrayal and isolation. But because of the resurrection, He made sure it doesn't have to last forever. In the end, Jesus was victorious over the cross, and God offers that victory to us too. Not just saving us from an eternity in hell, but in redeeming all of our traumas and mistakes."

"Redeeming our traumas," said Faye. She tilted her blond head to one side and looked at Amber critically. "I would have to say that you, dear one, are perhaps one of the best parts of my own trauma redemption."

Amber tucked a lock of hair behind her ear. "Why?"

"Because loving you was both very easy and very hard. When my Jamie died those many years ago, I didn't know if I'd ever be able to fully love another girl. At the time, loving Brittney was hard enough, although as time passed and my heart healed, I saw the great blessing she was to me. Still, I think, part of me wondered if I could love more than just Brittney. Or if I was even loving Brittney with everything I had."

Faye picked up the piece of foil and neatly folded it, smoothing out the edges. "Logan grew up and married, and while I love his wife dearly, they've always lived in Portland, and I didn't have to let her deep into my daily life."

"And then Frank brought you home that cold November morning. Everything in me wanted to wrap you up in my arms and protect you from the world. But you were determined to let me into only a tiny piece of your heart." Faye paused, lost in the memory.

"As I struggled to love you without overwhelming you," continued Faye, "I realized God had done a great work in me. I had been loving young ladies for years without hesitation. Not that any of them replaced my Jamie, but I finally understood that losing her wasn't holding me back from completely loving others."

Amber reached across the desk and grabbed Faye's hand. "You've been a wonderful Momma to me."

Faye put her other hand on top of Amber's. "Victory in the end."

"I don't know how God will redeem my past, but I do know this," said Amber. "I love a wonderful God, and He already has the victory I seek."

CHAPTER 12

ATRICIA CHECKED IN WITH BECKA, the receptionist at the clinic, and found a seat in the waiting room. The room was quiet. Apparently, no one in Crossing was presently in need of medical attention.

She could overhear Ryan talking in the back room.

"...trying different approaches. Amber's taking some sign language lessons, and he's starting to pick up a couple of the basic signs. And she and Peter are both trying to remember to get down on his level and talk directly facing him so he can see their lips."

Ryan and Dr. Williams stopped at the end of the hallway, just inside the waiting room.

"Sounds like good choices," said Dr. Williams. "Let me know if I can do anything."

"I will," said Ryan. "Have a good lunch. I'm just going to talk with Mrs. Guire here and get an update on how she's feeling."

John looked over at Patricia and, for the first time in years, she met his gaze. She stood, her mind desperately looking for something to say to him. "It's good to see you."

She wondered if he was surprised at her greeting. His face didn't show much. *Or maybe I just can't read him like I once could.*

He nodded briefly and walked to the front door. "I'll be back in about twenty minutes, Becka," he said.

"How about we go back here, Mrs. Guire?" said Ryan.

He led her into an exam room and pulled out the blood pressure cuff. As he fastened it around her arm, he asked, "So, how have things been going the last couple of weeks?"

"Better, I think."

He placed the thermometer in her ear and read the display. "Better as in the episodes are happening less frequently? Better as in they are less painful? Better how?"

"Yes," said Patricia hesitantly. "Shorter, I think."

Ryan made notes of her blood pressure and temperature. "Okay, so what else has changed?" He took the cuff from her arm and began to roll it up.

"What do you mean?"

"I mean, you tell me that things are getting better. And I just watched you look Dr. Williams in the eye and talk to him for the first time that I know of in the three plus years that he's been here."

She dismissed him with her hand as she looked away from him. "You see too much."

Ryan rolled the stool he sat on closer and leaned in with his elbows on his knees. "If we're talking about the health of my patients, that's what I get paid to do. If we're talking about the life of my friends, I'm just trying to help carry the load."

Patricia looked back at him, murmuring quietly, "Carry the burden."

"What burden?"

"That's what God said to me the other day when we were arguing." She caught Ryan's smirk. "Oh, please. Do you really think my relationship with God is that much different than my relationship with any of the rest of you?"

"I suppose not," said Ryan. "What burden was He talking about?"

"I don't know that I'm ready to share any of that with the likes of you." Patricia took in a deep breath. "I don't know that I'm ready to share it with anyone, quite honestly, but God's telling me to quit carrying the burden of my past alone."

"Okay. So what part can I carry?"

Patricia hesitated to answer. *Everything is about to change. I can't ever take this back if I say it out loud.* She took a deep breath and spit it out. "My Heather is alive. But she goes by a different name."

Ryan sat up. "You know where she is."

Patricia looked down at her hands, neatly folded in her lap. "Yes."

"You said she was adopted."

"Yes."

"Does she know?"

"No."

"Why not?"

"It was the choice of her adoptive parents. And me. To protect her."

"How does not telling her the truth of her birth protect her?"

Patricia could see the confusion on Ryan's face. *Can I make him understand?* She searched for the right words. "It's not so much the circumstances of her birth as it is her...conception."

There it was. The best she was able to do. She alternated between studying her folded hands and searching Ryan's face for signs of recognition.

"Mrs. Guire, are you telling me that you were..."

"Not a consenting adult," she interrupted.

"Dear Lord." Ryan leaned forward, folding his hands together as he placed his elbows on his knees.

"Yes, well, you can see that makes all this more difficult."

"How does Dr. Williams play into all this?"

Patricia suddenly realized how her confession on top of her past behavior might look. "He is innocent." She reached out and placed her hand on top of Ryan's. "Truly. He and I were considering marriage when…" She pulled back, folding her hands in her lap again. "…when *it* happened."

She slowly breathed in before continuing. "His career was really taking off. He was becoming very well known and highly respected."

"You didn't tell him."

She shook her head.

"No."

"Does he know anything? About the pregnancy? The child?"

"No. I left Portland shortly after I found out I was pregnant. That's when Jake took over the garage there."

"So Jake knows?"

"No. I told him I was sick and needed a few months away from the business."

Ryan stood and paced a couple steps away from her. "Mrs. Guire!"

Patricia wasn't sure what she expected from Ryan, but the look of shocked disbelief on his face was not it.

"Men, real men, want to know about these kinds of things. If anything like that had happened to Brittney, I would have stood by her side. I would have held her, loved her…been whatever she needed me to be."

"But the child wasn't his! And the affect to his career…"

"Look," said Ryan, sitting back down on the stool and rolling close to her. "I can't speak for the man John Williams was twenty-five years ago, but the man I know today wouldn't have cared about the genealogy of your baby girl or whatever people-with-more-money-than-sense would have thought. The man I know today would have only cared about you."

Patricia's mind was working overtime. *Have I looked at this wrong all these years? Would John have been there? Did I underestimate him?*

"And Jake. He might not have been able to do more than he did, but he would have cared. Knowing his reputation and the good job he's done all these years, he would have wanted to know." Ryan clenched his jaw. "I won't tell anyone or put any of this in your medical records. I will keep your confidence, but I encourage you to at least tell Dr. Williams. You need to know he's worried about you."

"Why do you say that?"

"As the doctor of record, he looks over all my case files. But he scrutinizes my care of you more closely than anyone else."

Patricia considered Ryan's simple statement. So much had just changed for her. She reached out, placing her hand on Ryan's cheek. "You are a good friend."

Ryan grinned back at her. "Mrs. Guire—are you going soft on me?"

She smiled back, patting his cheek. "I wouldn't count on it."

CHAPTER 13

*P*ATRICIA STOPPED IN FRONT IN FRONT of Jake's house, greeted by young Emma's bouncing light brown head. The natural wave in her hair curled under at her shoulders, making it look like someone spent a lot of time taming it, but the chaotic bangs revealed that she'd taken care of her own style this morning.

"You're here! You're here! You're here!"

Patricia laughed. "Yes, child. Did you think I wouldn't come this month as usual?"

"I knew you'd come, but the time between when you call and when you get here is always so very long," said Emma in her most dramatic voice.

Patricia gently held Emma's chin. "Would you rather I not call before I leave my house in Crossing?"

"I would rather you live right there!" Emma pointed to the house next door.

The child's desire for her to be close revived her spirit. "Ah. Perhaps one day, my sweet. You never know what God has planned for tomorrow."

Emma waited as Patricia took a bag out of the back seat then grabbed her hand as they walked to the door.

"Taylor has a surprise for you!" said Emma

"That you're not supposed to tell her about," said Jake.

Emma looked down at the sidewalk, "Oh, yeah."

Patricia walked up to the porch and greeted her friend with a hug. Jake held her back just a bit and looked critically at her face. "How are you?" he asked pointedly.

She smiled. "Better." She saw the questions in his eyes. "Truly. I will tell you more later."

"Did you forget me?" little Andrew called from inside the house.

Patricia looked through the door but could not see him. Jake spoke before she could ask her question.

"He's in his room until you got here."

"Another prank gone wrong?"

Jake rolled his eyes. "What else?" He held the door open for her and Emma as they walked inside. "He switched out the sugar that I use for my coffee."

"What did he switch it with?"

"Salt."

Patricia laughed. "Oh, Jake. It was a harmless prank."

"I know that. They always are. But as he becomes older, what if they aren't? What if he hurts someone?"

"What if he doesn't?" said Patricia, laying her hand on Jake's arm.

"You don't think I struggle over this?"

"I know you do," said Patricia. "But perhaps God simply wants you to enjoy your son's tendency toward fun while giving him boundaries to keep things safe?"

"How do I do that?"

Patricia's eyes sparkled. "Participate."

"Participate! You mean join in? Pull pranks on other people?"

"Why not? What is the downside?" she asked. Jake adjusted

his glasses while she continued. "You get access to his heart and mind, you can help him foresee dangerous possibilities, and you have fun with your son. I see no downside."

Emma pulled on Jake's shirt. "Daddy, can I participate too?" Her big eyes pleaded.

Jake roughed up her hair. "We'll see. Daddy has to think about this some more."

"Good morning," said Taylor, appearing in the doorway with a plate full of cinnamon rolls.

"Child, that smells delicious," said Patricia.

Taylor smiled. "I made them for you."

Andrew stuck his head around the corner. "Can I come out now? Nanna's here."

Patricia held out her arms to him, and he ran to hug her.

Everyone sat down to enjoy Taylor's rolls and the presents Patricia had for the kids. As Patricia and Jake cleaned up the dishes, Andrew ran outside to play with his new basketball while the girls went to Emma's room to hang her new glow-in-the-dark stars.

"Tell me more about your panic attacks," said Jake as he picked up the saucers. "What do you mean they are better?"

"They are going away," said Patricia. "They happen less often now." She grabbed the serving plate with just one remaining cinnamon roll on it.

"Will they eventually subside completely?"

"Although he can't be certain, Ryan thinks they will. At least, he says, they should once I have dealt with everything that brought them on to begin with."

"And are you working through all that in Shannon's Redemption Group?"

Patricia thought while she started running hot water in the sink. "Yes. Although I think I have more to do, people I need to talk to."

Jake waited silently, but Patricia could feel him watching her.

"One person I think I will talk to soon," said Patricia.

"And the other?"

"I cannot." Tears gathered in her eyes.

"Can't?" said Jake. "Or won't?"

Patricia blinked repeatedly, trying to keep the tears from taking over.

"I don't understand," said Jake.

"To talk to the other person would disrupt more lives than I have a right to."

"What are you talking about?" Jake turned off the water.

"Jake," said Patricia, reaching out to touch his hand. "It's okay. You don't need to worry."

"That's like telling me I don't have to breathe. Patricia, like it or not, you are part of our family. We love you, and with that comes all the emotions, including concern when we know something isn't right."

Patricia smiled. "I'm in good hands, my friend."

JAKE STOOD WATCHING PATRICIA DRIVE AWAY THE NEXT afternoon as the kids ran back inside the house. Yesterday had been a fairly normal day with her as they walked to a park and discussed business at the garage, and she'd helped Taylor make dinner. But in church services this morning, she'd been more withdrawn.

"What are you holding inside you, old woman?" he muttered to himself as she left his line of sight.

He considered his options, which seemed few. "God, what am I supposed to do? Am I just supposed to pray?"

That option didn't sit well with him, but he wasn't sure if it was because he wanted to do something or because God was directing him to do something. "Should I call Ryan? He probably can't tell me anything since she's seeing him as a patient."

Jake adjusted his glasses and breathed in deeply. "Give me guidance, Lord."

Dorothy.

"Her sister?"

Jake thought about the last time he'd talk to Dorothy, two Christmases ago. *Our first without Kelly, when the kids convinced Patricia to spend the day with us. Dorothy called to wish us all Merry Christmas.*

Before he changed his mind, Jake found her number in his address book and picked up the phone. She answered on the second ring.

"Dorothy? This is Jake Chaplain."

He could hear the confusion in her greeting.

"I don't know if your sister has been telling you anything, but I'm really concerned about her. I can't tell you much because she's not really sharing a lot with me..."

CHAPTER 14

*J*ULY THIRD. *FIVE WEEKS.* AMBER thought about the group sessions she and Patricia had attended throughout June. They were now more than halfway done with this special summer program, and she felt so very different from the woman who had first walked into Shannon's living room five weeks prior.

She shifted the bowl of watermelon in her lap and looked over at Peter. He was driving her and Patricia to group tonight. The ladies had decided to celebrate the 4th of July together with an evening picnic on their normal group night, inviting families to join them. She looked forward to introducing her husband to the woman who'd helped her so much.

Peter parked on the street near the house and took Daniel out of his car seat while Patricia and Amber grabbed the food they'd brought to share. Amber carefully balanced a tray of deviled eggs on top of the fragile, etched-glass bowl full of watermelon that Faye had sent.

Patricia led the way up the sidewalk, and Shannon greeted them at the door. "Come on in!" She inhaled deeply at Patricia's covered bowl of baked beans. "That smells wonderful!"

As Amber stepped inside, she turned to Shannon. "This is my husband, Peter."

Shannon grasped Peter's hand warmly and then turned her attention to Daniel. "Hey, cutie!" She tickled his belly and smiled in delight as he grinned at her from the safety of Peter's neck. "A little bit shy, are we?"

"Just a little," said Peter.

Patricia returned from dropping her food off in the kitchen and reached out to Daniel. "Let me take the little one while you go meet the others." Daniel eyed Shannon cautiously while leaning towards Patricia.

Shannon led the way to the kitchen. "Most everyone is outside around the grill, but you are welcome to hang out here in the kitchen if you'd prefer. Oh, honey, I'd like you to meet…"

The bowl in Amber's hands crashed to the floor, watermelon going everywhere. Time froze as she met the eyes of the man Shannon had just called "honey." *No!*

Her knees almost buckled on her, and she might have fallen if Peter hadn't been so close. She vaguely felt his hands on her shoulders. Voices sounded like she was underwater. She took a step back, running more firmly into Peter. She turned and forced her way through obstacles, her focus on escape through the front door.

The Jeep. I have to get to the Jeep.

Someone yelled her name, but she didn't stop. She powered through the front door, running as fast as she could to the Jeep. *Peter's Jeep.*

Strong arms caught her halfway across the yard. They held tight as she struggled, fists pounding on a solid chest. Tears flooded her eyes as soft words slowly made their way into her brain.

"I've got you, my Ray," said Peter. "You're safe."

Peter. Slowly, her body relaxed. *Peter.* She clenched his shirt and focused. *I am safe. He can't hurt me.*

As she stopped fighting him, Peter eased his hold on her. His chin on the top of her head, one hand gently ran down her hair as she regained control.

He leaned back slightly and kissed her forehead. He took both hands, smoothing her hair from around her face, wiping tears from her cheeks. "Are you ready to tell me what that was about?"

Amber looked at the small group gathered in front of Shannon's house as she laid her head against Peter: Patricia holding Daniel, Debbie, Lynn, and a child she assumed was one of Lynn's children. Women she'd grown to care about through this group. Shannon was not there, probably cleaning up the mess of glass and fruit she'd just made in the kitchen.

"That man, Peter," she whispered.

"Shannon's husband?"

Amber nodded. "That was Martin."

Amber felt Peter tense. She leaned into his strength even more, and his arms tightened around her.

After several minutes, Peter broke the silence. "What do you want to do? Do you want to go home?"

The battled raged in Amber's mind. She wanted to be as far away from Martin as possible, yet his presence in Shannon's peace-filled home confused her. *Daddy! What do I do?*

A gentle voice responded. *What does Psalm 56 tell you?*

Amber concentrated on the Psalm she'd been studying. "When I am afraid," she said, "I will trust in You. In God, whose word I praise, in God I trust; I will not be afraid. What can mortal man do to me?"

"Your Psalm?" said Peter.

Amber sighed. "Yes." She thought for a moment before adding, "I want to go home, Peter, but I need to tell Shannon. I can't leave without seeing her."

Peter stepped back, his hands framing her face. "Okay. But we go together."

Amber cleared her throat and faced the group still standing on the front step. As she approached, Patricia looked at her questioningly. Amber reached out to her. "I need to go home."

Patricia simply nodded. "I will put Daniel in his car seat."

Lynn reached out to hug Amber, great concern in her eyes. Amber returned the hug and smiled at Debbie as she and Peter walked into the house.

Martin stood in the hallway, tears streaming down his face. She stopped abruptly when she saw him, leaning back into Peter for security.

"Amber," said Martin. "I'm so sorry."

Shannon appeared behind Martin as Amber focused on not running. Martin gestured with his hands, and Amber instinctively flinched. Peter quietly reached out on both sides of her, wrapping his hands around her upper arms.

Martin looked down at his hands and then dropped them to his sides. Shannon placed a hand on his forearm, concern for him filling her posture.

"I have no excuse," Martin finally said. "And I know it's asking a lot, but I ask for your forgiveness."

Amber raised her chin slightly.

Forgiveness. Such a simple word but so full of meaning. She considered her journey over the last five weeks and realized all of it was truly about repentance and forgiveness. *Everything about the Christian life comes down to repentance and forgiveness. Can I offer that to him?*

Can you not? came the gentle reply.

Amber looked back at Peter. She grabbed hold of one of his hands and held tight. "Obviously I still have a lot of work to do, but I can't deny the work that God's already done. I have forgiven you, Martin…"

He took a step forward, and she held her hand out to stop him.

"…Not that I want any kind of relationship with you."

Martin nodded. "Fair enough."

Amber focused on Shannon, still holding on to her husband. "I hope you understand, but we can't stay."

Shannon walked towards her. "Of course." She hugged Amber tight. "I'm so sorry. I had no idea my Nick was your Martin."

Amber hugged her back but felt empty. The closeness she had been feeling towards her earlier was now in question. "It's okay. You couldn't have known."

Shannon released Amber. "Call me if…well, if you want to."

Amber smiled at her. She took one last look at Martin before turning to walk out the door.

CHAPTER 15

*A*MBER PINCHED THE BRIDGE OF her nose. The brisk walk out to the river near their house had expended her anger but done little to soothe her. The leaves on the trees rustled in the breeze above her as the sunshine struggled to peak through the clouds on an otherwise warm July afternoon.

She walked over to the wood bench Peter had made for his mother and focused on the verse he'd inscribed along the back. *The Lord has chosen you to be his treasured possession.*

"I'm not much of a treasure today, Lord," she muttered.

"I disagree with that."

Amber looked to her left. "Hey, Pete," she said quietly.

He walked closer to her but didn't say anything.

Guilt for losing her temper on him and Chad at the office a few moments ago overwhelmed her. "I'm sorry I exploded on you and Chad."

"How about you tell me what's really going on, because I don't believe this is all about the log counts being off."

She tucked a lock of hair behind her ear. "I'm not sure."

Peter stepped closer, taking her hands in his. "Yes, I think you know."

"Ahhhh." Amber twisted free and plopped on the bench, placing her elbows on her knees and burying her face in her hands. "Why does this have to be so hard?"

"What?"

He wouldn't settle for less than what was weighing on her heart. *I shouldn't settle for less either.* "I don't know if I can go back to Shannon's group."

Peter sat down beside her.

"Why not?"

"You know," she said.

"I know the part I'm struggling with," said Peter. "I want to hear what you're struggling with."

Amber looked sideways at him. "You're having trouble with this?"

"Oh, no. You are not redirecting this conversation to me. You've snapped at me four times in the last six days. It's time we deal with this."

"I've been really horrible, haven't I?"

"No. Challenging," said Peter with a grin to take the edge off his words.

Amber smiled back before leaning with her back against him. "I'm sorry."

He kissed the back of her head. "It's okay. Now 'fess up. What's going through your head?"

Amber sighed deeply. "I don't believe Shannon knew that her husband and I had a past, but now I think that every time I walk into her house, I'll be thinking about him and not the group or what I'm supposed to be doing."

"Do you think he'll interrupt the group?"

"No. At least, he never did before."

"So you're concerned that you'll be more focused on your past than on your present."

"That almost makes it sound silly," said Amber.

"No, it's not," said Peter, wrapping both arms around her.

"Maybe I don't understand the group right, but I thought the point was to look at whatever traumas you've experienced and investigate them with God at your side."

"Yeah, I guess. We've been encouraged to look at the lies we've believed and let God speak fresh truth into them. For me, that meant giving up the lie that God wasn't there or didn't care."

"So how is you going to group meeting and thinking about your traumatic past with Martin a bad thing?"

Amber thought about Peter's take on her dilemma. "You really think I should go?"

Peter turned her around so she could see his face. "I want you as far away from that man and his home as possible." Peter ran his hand through his hair, a sign Amber recognized as building frustration or concern. "But," Peter continued, "that's not what God wants."

"Why do you say that?" Amber really wanted to know whether returning to her Redemption Group was the right decision before her next meeting tomorrow night.

"I've watched you over the last week slowly rewrap yourself in the cloak of shame. In these six days, I've heard more self-condemnation come from your mouth about yourself than I've heard in years. Suddenly, in your own words, you are incomepetent, disorganized, and horrible."

"Seeing him again really got to me."

Peter pulled her in close. "I get that. I do. You should be angry and hurt over what he did to you. It's okay to feel that fear and horror as you walk through this process of dealing with it all."

He released her, using a hand to tilt her chin up so they were looking in each other's eyes. "But my beautiful Ray, you cannot live there. I long for you to grab hands with God, walk through the pain, and leave the burden of it behind you."

Tears began to form as she thought about what Peter was asking of her.

"I know those days will forever be in your memory," said Peter, "and I know they help explain why you do or say or think certain ways." He rubbed a thumb across her cheek, wiping away a tear. "But they don't have to define the rest of your life."

She shook her head. "I don't know if I can do that."

"Do you trust God?"

The hesitation was very slight. "Yes."

"Then quit looking at the end of the road and just focus on today."

Amber sighed. She looked at her small hand safely clasped inside Peter's. "Psalm 56 says that my enemies will turn back when I call for help."

"Are you thinking about Martin?"

Amber smiled and met Peter's eyes. "No. I'm thinking about shame. Shame is my enemy, and with God at my side, it will turn back."

"That's my girl."

AMBER SAT DOWN ON THE COUCH AFTER PUTTING DANIEL TO BED for the evening and breathed in deeply. Chad had graciously accepted her apology. The rest of the day had gone smoothly. Daniel's tooth had finally made its appearance, and the child was seeming more like himself and easier to put to bed.

She was just beginning to think about whether or not she would attend the group meeting tomorrow when the phone rang.

"Hello, child," said Patricia. "I just wanted to check on you."

The gesture warmed Amber's heart.

"Shouldn't I be the one checking on you?"

"I was not the one who most recently had a great shock."

Amber snuggled deeper into the couch cushions. "I'm okay, or maybe I'm getting to be okay."

"Yes," said Patricia, "I can understand that. I didn't think you would want to go tomorrow."

Amber paused. "I've been thinking a lot about that."

"You need to do what you think is best for you."

"No, I don't think so," said Amber. "I need to do what God wants me to do."

"Hmm. Yes, you are right."

"Will you pick me up about the usual time?"

"I will see you then."

Amber hung up the phone, thinking about her conversation with Patricia.

"You know what?" said Peter.

She turned to look at her husband standing just outside the kitchen, still holding a hand towel from cleaning up.

He tossed the towel onto the counter, walked over to her, and leaned down, placing one hand on the back of the couch on either side of her. "I think you are the bravest woman I know." He kissed the tip of her nose.

"I sure don't feel brave."

"'My grace is sufficient for you,'" Peter quoted from 2 Corinthians, "'for my power is made perfect in weakness. Therefore I will boast all the more gladly about my weaknesses, so that Christ's power may rest on me.'"

CHAPTER 16

MBER SAT IN PATRICIA'S SILENT vehicle. She wasn't sure how many minutes had passed since they'd first pulled up, but she knew it was close to time for the group to start.

"We probably look ridiculous," said Amber.

"Sitting in a car is not the silliest thing I've done in my life," said Patricia.

"I feel..." Amber struggled to find the right word. "Vulnerable."

"You are."

"So what do I do?"

"Do you believe God wanted you here tonight?"

"Yes," said Amber quietly.

"Then it is simple. Either proceeding forward in obedience is worth the cost right now, or you will pay the cost of disobedience later."

Amber couldn't help the brief laughter that burst from her. She looked at the old woman who was becoming a dear friend. "That's one of the things I love about you, Patricia Guire."

Patricia raised her eyebrows as if she had no idea what Amber was talking about.

"You don't mince words. You say it like you think it, and I am rarely left wondering how you feel."

Patricia patted Amber's arm. "I'm sure many people would agree with you, but the truth is that I've left too many things unsaid in my past. Too many times I kept my mouth shut, playing the part of a martyr, when in reality I was simply too prideful to let people really know me."

"Wow. That's quite a revelation."

"Yes, and I'm seeing more clearly every day that I owe many people apologies. All these years I felt justified in my pain, never recognizing that I made decisions without giving the people that my decisions affected any choice in the matter. They did it my way, or they got left behind." Patricia took a deep breath. "Sometimes my decision left them behind without offering them an alternative. I've been very selfish, only giving of myself on my terms." She looked at Amber. "Including you, child."

"Me?"

"Yes. I've watched you from afar since shortly after you came to Crossing, jealous of Faye and the relationship she got to cultivate with you. But the reality is that I never asked much of you. Never let you know I wanted more."

Patricia played with the straps on the purse sitting in her lap. "Truth is, I'm lonely. I'd like more people—more friends—in my life." Patricia looked Amber in the eye. "I'd be honored if one of those people was you."

Amber smiled and grabbed Patricia's hand. "Oh, Mrs. Guire. I'm the one that's honored. I'd love to be considered your friend."

"Good," said Patricia. "Now, do we go in, or do we sneak away and get some ice cream?"

Amber smiled. "As tempting as that is…" she sighed before continuing. "We go in. The cost of disobedience is too high."

"Then quit stalling, child, and get out of the car."

"Yes, ma'am."

Amber led the way to the front door, her stomach growing more nervous with every step. She quietly knocked on the door and waited.

Shannon opened the door, and tears immediately sprung to her eyes. "I wasn't sure you would come tonight!"

"I wasn't either," said Amber. "Are we still welcome?"

"Please." Shannon stood to the side, allowing room for Amber and Patricia to pass by her.

"Amber, can I talk to you a minute?" Shannon asked.

Amber smiled at Patricia and nodded that she should go ahead to the living room without her. She quietly waited for Shannon to continue. She'd never seen the group leader so anxious.

"After everyone left last week," Shannon said, "Nick and I had a long talk. I knew when we got married that he'd been a very different man, a cruel man in many respects, before he trusted his life to Jesus. But that never seemed real to me because I've only known who he is now." Shannon wrung her hands. "When I realized last week that the stories you'd told in group were about my husband, well, I really didn't know what to think."

Amber wasn't sure what to think of this confession from Shannon. "It's okay. I've never once thought you knew beforehand."

Shannon smiled at her. "I know I can't apologize, shouldn't apologize, for his behavior. But I am sorry for all the pain you've been through. I'm just not sure... I guess that before last week happened, I was hoping that after the group ended, you and I could still be friends. But now I feel like that's too much to ask of you."

Amber stepped closer and reached out to touch Shannon's tightly clasped hands. "How about we just take it slow? I would love to keep up with you, and maybe, in little pieces at first, you could introduce me to this new Nick."

Shannon looked at her with hope in her eyes. "Really?"

Amber smiled back. "I think, under different circumstances, I might really like him."

"From what I know, Jesus has done a miraculous work in him. I'd love to tell you more."

"It may be a long while before I'm ready to see him again."

"What you are offering is more than I dared hope for, Amber. Thank you."

LATER THAT EVENING, PATRICIA CLOSED HER FRONT DOOR AND walked into her front room. She looked around at the trinkets she'd collected over the years, buying them from people who couldn't pay the full price to fix their vehicles at her garages. Some she'd paid far more than they were worth, but the satisfaction of help-ing a person in need always made up the difference.

Until the last year or so.

Things filled her home. Memories of kindness. Moments of generosity. She touched a small statuette of a girl worth at least a hundred dollars to a collector. Beside it sat a sixty-year-old mantle clock, and beside that a decorative vase from a top New York store.

But they were all from the past, and all from strangers. She'd given up her future long ago—selflessly, she'd thought back then. Now she knew the truth.

Pride stood fully before her. And it was ugly.

She'd never given the man she claimed to love a chance. She'd decided for him that his career was more important to him than she was, that his esteem more important than a child.

I decided he couldn't possibly love a child who wasn't his.

And the child? a gentle voice asked.

Perhaps giving her up was the right thing, but I did it for the wrong reasons as well. And I've never given her the chance to fully know her heritage.

A heritage of love, said the voice.

I've always focused on the shame, thought Patricia.

She sighed deeply. "No more."

Her thoughts turned to Amber and their conversation in the car. "Amber is right. The cost of disobedience is too high." She looked around the room, seeing nothing but tables overflowing with junk. "God, help me. Help me to fix this. Help me to do all You ask."

CHAPTER 17

ATRICIA LOOKED IN THE MIRROR. She couldn't remember the last time she cared this much about her clothes. The green shirt with tiny white flowers was neatly pressed and tucked into her blue jeans. "Well, that's about as good as I'm going to get."

She went to the kitchen and looked for the fifth time at the contents of the small picnic basket on her counter, glancing around to see if anything else came to mind.

A thought planted itself as her anxiety grew. Maybe tomorrow would be better.

"No," she told herself. In her efforts to avoid John around town, she'd learned his habits fairly well. "He eats at the diner on Fridays. It's either today or wait until next week."

She closed the lid with a snap, thrust her arm through the handles, and began the short walk to the clinic.

When she entered the small building, Becka greeted her, but Patricia's eyes were focused on Dr. Williams, who stood at the counter writing notes in a file.

He looked up and met her gaze. After a moment, he said, "I suspect you are looking for Ryan. I'll get him for you."

"Actually," she said as he took a step away, "I came to see you."

She thought she recognized a small sign of shock in his eyes, but he maintained his composure.

"Would you like to talk in private?"

"Please."

He motioned for her to lead the way down the hallway to the exam rooms. Ryan stood quietly in the doorway, and as she passed him, she paused to fold her hand over his.

She put the basket on the exam table and turned to face the doctor. He closed the door behind him but did not step further inside the room than was necessary.

I deserve that, she thought. Uncertain where to begin, she blurted out, "I brought you lunch."

"Lunch?"

"Yes. An Italian sub, homemade potato salad, some lemonade, and a slice of cake."

His brow creased, and she watched the battle going on across his face. He'd been a man of few words when they'd dated. *Perhaps he's grown even more quiet over the years.*

"I have no idea what you like anymore, but I remembered you used to like sub sandwiches."

"Why?"

"Because you need to eat."

"Patricia."

Her name. She wasn't sure whether he thundered it in frustration or whispered it in hope. Just hearing her name cross his lips was enough to break her resolve of holding everything together. Tears gathered as she struggled to speak a coherent sentence. She could continue to drag this out and merely answer his questions, or she could openly tell him why she was really here.

"I owe you an apology and an explanation, not that I deserve you listening to either one."

He didn't stop her, so she kept going.

"Years ago, I ran away from you because something had happened to me, and I couldn't let the shame of it discredit you in any way. I realize now how wrong I was to leave you out of the decision. I am sorry for that."

"I'm not sure you're making any sense."

Patricia sighed. *So much for getting out of this the easy way. Lord, give me strength.* "Perhaps we could sit so I can tell you the story."

John moved the two chairs in the room closer together, and they sat. He never interrupted her as she laid her pain out before him. He listened patiently, his eyes never leaving her face until the very end. As she fell silent, he closed his eyes.

"Can you ever forgive me?" Patricia whispered.

John looked at her, reaching his arm out to grasp the back of her chair. "Can you forgive me?"

"You?"

"My sweet, did you really think I didn't know how to find you? I knew about your relationship with your sister, how close you were, and I knew that if you didn't run straight to her, she would know how to get a message to you."

He cleared his throat. "But my own pride kept me from tracking you down. I was so hurt that you left without even leaving me a note, that I buried myself in my work and pretended it didn't matter."

"So now what do we do?"

"How about we start with me enjoying the lunch a dear friend brought to me today?"

Friend. She grasped her hands together in her lap so she wouldn't push her luck by touching him before he was ready. "I like that."

He covered her hands with his own, hesitating briefly for a moment before saying, "And how about I treat you to dinner at the diner for your birthday on Saturday?"

Patricia was shocked. "You remember my birthday?"

He looked embarrassed. "And the anniversary of our first date in late August, and the date I asked you to marry me in May."

She smiled at him. "I'm thankful you decided to come to Crossing, John."

"Me too, my sweet."

His use of her old nickname gave her great hope for their future.

DINNER PASSED QUICKLY THAT SATURDAY AS JOHN AND PATRICIA caught each other up on the last several years of their lives. The sun was just beginning to fade as they walked back to her house.

"Why did you never marry, John?"

"I poured my life into the kids at the hospital. I became obsessed with finding the best treatment plans, gleaning every bit of knowledge I could from all the latest research in the field. I was determined to give all my kids the best chance I could." He shrugged. "That doesn't leave time for much else."

"And tends to lead to burn out."

"Yes. I think that's part of why Crossing appealed to me. After pushing myself so hard for so many years, the thought of nothing more strenuous than ankle sprains and seasonal flus seemed almost relaxing."

They walked in companionable silence until they were almost at Patricia's home.

"Do you know that car?" said John with some concern in his voice.

Patricia looked towards her house and saw her sister's silver Ford Taurus in the driveway. "What is Dorothy doing here?"

"Your sister?"

Patricia nodded as she quickened her steps.

As they made the turn up the front walk, Patricia saw someone sitting on one of the chairs on her porch. The hair was too dark and long to be her sister. "Melody?" Patricia rushed forward. "Is everything okay? Your mother? David?"

Melody smiled. "Don't worry, Aunt Patty, everyone is good. David's in the field right now training for deployment. And when I left Mom's this afternoon, she was fine."

Patricia relaxed, gave Melody a hug, and introduced John.

"I think I should leave you two alone to catch up," he said.

"Perhaps we can all have dinner one night next week," said Patricia. She looked at Melody. "How long are you planning on staying?"

"Well, that all depends," said Melody.

Patricia expected to hear something about David's training or Dorothy's constantly changing plans. Her sister could be a tad flighty.

Melody glanced at John, then back at Patricia. "Aunt Patty, I've talked to Mom and she's told me what she knows. I'd really like to hear it from you."

Patricia felt like she couldn't breathe. Her heartbeat echoed in her ears as her brain scrambled for some explanation other than what she feared.

"I'd really like to know more," said Melody hesitantly, "about the circumstances of my birth and why you gave me up for adoption to your sister."

CHAPTER 18

P ATRICIA'S KNEES ABOUT GAVE WAY underneath her, and she felt John's arm surround her.

"Whoa, there. Let's have a seat right here."

John guided her to the camel back rocking chair next to the one Melody had been sitting in.

"Aunt Patty?"

"Patricia, are you in any pain?" She felt John press against her wrist as he checked her pulse.

"I'm okay," she managed to say.

"I'll get her something to drink," said Melody.

Melody dug through Patricia's purse and found the keys before disappearing inside. John sat in the chair beside her.

"You don't feel any pain?"

"No," said Patricia.

"Is it hard to breathe?"

Patricia tried to take a deep breath. "Only a little."

"Here's some lemonade," said Melody, pressing a glass in her hand.

"Thank you, child."

Patricia took a sip more because she felt like they expected her to drink than because she truly wanted some at that moment.

"Is she okay?"

"Yes, I think she'll be fine," said John. "It's just a minor panic attack. You're staying the night?"

"Yes," said Melody.

"I'll leave you my number. If she starts having severe chest pain or more trouble breathing, call me."

Patricia watched Melody pull her cell phone out and type in John's information.

"Tonight," he said, "she needs rest and gentle care."

"I'll watch over her," Melody promised.

John stopped in front of Patricia. "Call me if you need me."

She nodded. "Thank you."

As John walked away from the house, Melody sat down beside Patricia. "I'm sorry I shocked you. I suppose that wasn't the best way to approach the subject."

"How did you find out?"

"Jake was worried about you, and he called Mom. The poor man is very confused, but he was able to give her enough details that she figured it all out. Why didn't you tell us you've been sick?"

"I'm not really sick."

Melody grimaced. "Aunt Patty."

"They are just panic attacks."

"Were you having them last fall when David and I came?"

Patricia thought for a moment about skirting the truth. *Pride doesn't give in easily, Lord.* "Yes."

"And they are all about me?"

Patricia reached out and grabbed Melody's hand. "No, child. They are all about me—trying to deny truth for too long."

"I have questions."

"Go ahead and ask. Anything you want to know. I owe you that much."

"Aunt Patty, don't you see? You've already given me so much. You gave me life. You made sure I was protected and loved. You walked with me while my child died. And then you took me in while I was hurting and only wanted to hurt others."

Patricia's eyes filled with tears. "I could not do less."

"I can't imagine the sacrifices my life has cost you."

"You listen to me. You are a blessing. The sacrifices I made were largely self-imposed and caused more pain. About the only good decision I made during those months was to give birth to you."

They sat in silence for a few moments, and Patricia enjoyed the multi-colored sky as the sun set and night took over. The crickets were beginning to sing their chorus, and Patricia thought she heard an owl in the distance.

"Why? Why give me to your sister?"

Patricia took a deep breath, allowing herself to remember the heart-wrenching days as she let Dorothy become Melody's mom. "Because I didn't think I would be the mother you needed, but I couldn't take the chance on giving you to a family I didn't know. I wanted to be a part of your life, no matter how small that part might be."

"Mom said you were the one who named me."

"After one of my favorite flowers." Patricia smiled. "That plant down there on the corner of the porch…"

"The one with the little pink bells?"

"Yes. Most people call it Mediterranean pink heather, although it's really a heath plant." Patricia shifted in her chair slightly before continuing. "It's a small plant, never growing much more than about twelve inches tall, but it's strong. It not only survives the tough Northwest winters, but it usually blooms before spring arrives."

"That explains my middle name, but why Melody?"

"Because that plant is also full of life. Animals love its sweet flowers and dense ground cover, so a song of one type or another is always coming from it, depending on who's nestled into it."

"That's quite a lot to live up to."

"The circumstances of your conception may have been horrid, but I knew God had a plan for you. And I wanted to give you the best foundation I could."

Melody squeezed Patricia's hand. "You did a good job, Aunt Patty."

"You aren't hurt or angry?"

Melody shook her head. "No. I wonder what would be different if I'd have grown up with you as a mother instead of Mom. But I'm okay with it all. God wasn't surprised by any of this. He knew the choices we would each make, and He's working it out for our good."

"Dorothy did a good job with you."

"I suspect she had a lot of prayer support happening here in Crossing."

Patricia smiled. "Come on. I have some cake inside. We can eat while you catch me up on what's happened with you since you left here last November."

Melody reached out to help Patricia stand. "And I can tell you all about the baby."

"Baby?"

Melody smiled. "I'm seven weeks pregnant."

CHAPTER 19

*M*ATTHEW STOOD AT THE CORNER watching Melody tell Patricia the baby news. He smiled as they hugged, rejoicing at the work the Father had accomplished in each of their lives.

"The old one still has a long way to go," said Michael, appearing suddenly beside Matthew, his golden curls bobbing in the wind.

"Yes," said Matthew as he turned to face him, "but she is moving again. And her secrets are revealed to some of those she most loves."

Michael nodded. "The enemy has been effectively pushed back here." He watched as Matthew crouched down to pet an orange tabby that rubbed up against their blue jeans. "You did well."

Matthew thought about his moments with the various people of this town, the battles he'd helped them face in the enemy's desire to destroy them. "They found their hope."

"And it brought the Father great glory."

Matthew watched as Melody and Patricia walked inside. He had confidence in what God had worked out in each of them, as well as what God had done in the hearts of the Yagers and Griffins. None of them would be easily shaken again.

"You have a new assignment," said Michael.

Matthew stood and blew a bit of cat hair from his hands. "Here?"

"Portland."

BIBLIOGRAPHY

Lewis B. Smedes was an author, ethicist, and theologian. He taught as a professor for over two decades at Fuller Theological Seminary, Pasadena, California. He died in 2002.

Chapter 9, Lewis Smedes quote

Justin and Lindsey Holcomb, *Rid of My Disgrace* (Wheaton, Illinois: Crossway, 2011), 21% through eBook.

From the bibliography of *Rid of My Disgrace*: Lewis B. Smedes, *Shame and Grace* (San Francisco: HarperCollins, 1993), 80.

RECOMMENDED RESOURCES

The following two books used in Redemption Groups are referred to by Amber and Patricia throughout Crossing's Redemption.

Redemption: Freed by Jesus from the Idols We Worship and the Wounds We Carry by Mike Wilkerson, 2011

Rid of My Disgrace: Hope and Healing for Victims of Sexual Assault by Justin and Lindsey Holcomb, 2011

VERSES TO CONSIDER

In Crossing's Redemption, Faye offers to write down some verses for Amber that speak to how precious people are to God. I encourage you to do a search for yourself, but here are a few to get you started.

From the New International Version

Genesis 1:26–27 Then God said, "Let us make mankind in our image, in our likeness, so that they may rule over the fish in the sea and the birds in the sky, over the livestock and all the wild animals, and over all the creatures that move along the ground." So God created mankind in his own image, in the image of God he created them; male and female he created them.

Deuteronomy 7:6 For you are a people holy to the Lord your God. The Lord your God has chosen you out of all the peoples

on the face of the earth to be his people, his treasured possession.

Psalm 139:13–16 For you created my inmost being; you knit me together in my mother's womb. I praise you because I am fearfully and wonderfully made; your works are wonderful, I know that full well. My frame was not hidden from you when I was made in the secret place, when I was woven together in the depths of the earth. Your eyes saw my unformed body; all the days ordained for me were written in your book before one of them came to be.

Psalm 149:4 The Lord takes delight in his people.

John 10:10 The thief comes only to steal and kill and destroy; I have come that they may have life, and have it to the full.

John 14:15–18 [Jesus speaking] "If you love me, keep my commands. And I will ask the Father, and he will give you another advocate to help you and be with you forever—the Spirit of truth. The world cannot accept him, because it neither sees him nor knows him. But you know him, for he lives with you and will be in you. I will not leave you as orphans; I will come to you.

2 Corinthians 12:9 [The Lord] said to me, "My grace is sufficient for you, for my power is made perfect in weakness." Therefore I will boast all the more gladly about my weaknesses, so that Christ's power may rest on me.

Ephesians 2:10 For we are God's handiwork, created in Christ Jesus to do good works, which God prepared in advance for us to do.

Colossians 1:21–23 Once you were alienated from God and were enemies in your minds because of your evil behavior. But now he has reconciled you by Christ's physical body through death to present you holy in his sight, without blemish and free from accusation—if you continue in your faith, established and firm, and do not move from the hope held out in the gospel.

Hebrews 4:13–16 Nothing in all creation is hidden from God's sight. Everything is uncovered and laid bare before the eyes of him to whom we must give account.

Therefore, since we have a great high priest who has ascended into heaven, Jesus the Son of God, let us hold firmly to the faith we profess. For we do not have a high priest who is unable to empathize with our weaknesses, but we have one who has been tempted in every way, just as we are—yet he did not sin. Let us then approach God's throne of grace with confidence, so that we may receive mercy and find grace to help us in our time of need.

1 John 3:1–2 See what great love the Father has lavished on us, that we should be called children of God! And that is what we are! The reason the world does not know us is that it did not know him. Dear friends, now we are children of God, and what we will be has not yet been made known. But we know that when Christ appears, we shall be like him, for we shall see him as he is.

DID YOU LIKE THE BOOK?

Would you please leave a review with your favorite bookstore or book club?

Want more from Carrie Daws? Check out all the book related Freebies available at CarrieDaws.com. You'll find book club discussion guides, additional short stories, and more!

Want even more? Carrie loves to support and talk with Christian readers! Not only does she personally respond to every email she receives, but she writes weekly devotions based on themes within her books. Check it out on CarrieDaws.com!

ABOUT THE AUTHOR

God rewrote Carrie's dreams from being a corporate accountant to an author. With a background writing devotions, a mentor encouraged her to think bigger. The writing monster she now barely keeps contained was born.

After ten years in the US Air Force, Carrie's husband medically retired, and they settled in North Carolina. With their three children figuring out what they want to do in life after school, Carrie stays busy keeping up with her family, loving on women, and reading as much as she can.

For more information about Carrie, please visit CarrieDaws.com.

ALSO BY CARRIE DAWS

FICTION BOOKS

Embers Series

Kindling Embers

Igniting Embers

Extinguishing Embers

Sacred Trust Series

Seeking Isabel

Finding Benjamin

Banishing Felipe

Home Front Heroines Series

More Than Meets the Eye

Not My Ways

ALSO BY CARRIE DAWS
NONFICTION BOOKS

The Warrior's Bride: Biblical Strategies to Help the Military Spouse Thrive

Beyond Warrior's Bride Series: Your Extended Family, Reintegration, Moving, Finances, Other Military Spouses, Retirement

I've Got Jesus . . . Now What?

Annual Prayer Journal (Free at CarrieDaws.com!)

Living in the Shadow of Death: Learning to Thrive through Tragedy and Uncertainty

Mentoring for Life (Free at CarrieDaws.com!)

www.ingramcontent.com/pod-product-compliance
Lightning Source LLC
Chambersburg PA
CBHW030546130626
46552CB00006B/2455